THE
VANISHING
OF
DR WINTER

A POSIE PARKER MYSTERY #4

L. B. HATHAWAY

WHITEHAVEN

WHITEHAVEN MAN PRESS

London

First published in Great Britain in 2016
by Whitehaven Man Press, London

Copyright © L.B. Hathaway 2016
(http://www.lbhathaway.com, email: permissions@lbhathaway.com)
The moral right of the author, L.B. Hathaway, has been asserted.

A CIP catalogue record for this book is available
from the British Library.

ISBN (e-book:) 978-0-9929254-5-1
ISBN (paperback:) 978-0-9929254-6-8

Jacket illustration by Red Gate Arts.
Formatting and design by J.D. Smith.

For Ray and Tine,
whose story goes on

By L.B. Hathaway

The Posie Parker Mystery Series

1. *Murder Offstage: A Posie Parker Mystery*

2. *The Tomb of the Honey Bee: A Posie Parker Mystery*

3. *Murder at Maypole Manor: A Posie Parker Mystery*

4. *The Vanishing of Dr Winter: A Posie Parker Mystery*

PART ONE
Monday 18th and
Tuesday 19th December, 1922

One

(Cambridge, 1922)

Felicity Fyne had never asked for help from anyone. But desperate times called for desperate measures.

She shifted uncomfortably from foot to foot on the freezing slushy pavement and stared through the fogged-up window of the Belgian chocolate shop in All Saints Passage. It was the finest chocolate shop in Cambridge, and she watched the girl inside, the only customer, choosing a half-kilo of fresh cream truffles with obvious delight.

Felicity had followed the girl here on purpose; down Trinity Street and through the crowded craft market, past the shops with all their gaudy Christmas decorations on display. And now here she was. Felicity swallowed hard. Never in a blue moon would she have imagined she would have had to resort to *this*. Spying. And stalking.

The girl inside, a neat brunette with very short hair, was wearing a dark red beret and a matching woollen coat with white piping. Fairly nice things, Felicity thought to herself with reluctant approval; expensive but not showy. The girl was laughing at something the shop assistant was saying. Felicity strained to hear the conversation through the thin glass:

'No. My gosh, don't bother wrapping it up! It's for me, a present to myself. I know, I'm a terrible greedy pig.'

Yes, Felicity thought, that would be about right. She remembered that the girl had had a very sweet tooth and an insatiable appetite. She hadn't changed much in five years, then. Plumper, perhaps, but not worse for it. Certainly better dressed than the last time they'd met in France, but that wasn't hard. Oh, and more famous, of course. But the same girl nonetheless. She was even holding that same wretched carpet bag.

Suddenly, in a flurry of shopping bags the brunette stepped out of the shop doorway into the dark passageway. It was now or never.

Felicity called out from the shadowy tangle of frozen trees and chained-up bicycles where she was loitering.

'Miss Parker? Miss Posie Parker?'

She saw the girl blink blindly into the darkness.

'Who's there?' the brunette called out nervously, clutching her enormous carpet bag tightly to her body. The green-coloured box of chocolates quivered in her hand.

Felicity stepped into the oblong of light cast by the shop window.

'You might not remember me, Miss Parker?' She took off her smart veiled black hat and let the light fall fully on her finely-boned face, revealing very blonde hair drawn up into a tight unfashionable bun in the style of at least five years ago.

'It's Felicity Fyne. *Sister* Fyne, as was. I'm sorry to startle you. But we worked together in the war: 1917, Arras. Casualty Clearing Station Number 8. You drove ambulances, and I was a nurse. A professional nurse.'

The brunette stared curiously and in a none-too-friendly fashion. Felicity extended a leather-gloved hand with a formality she normally reserved only for people much older or richer than herself. Posie Parker seemed to wait a jot more than was quite socially acceptable before shaking hands, and Felicity felt a quick tremor of hostility pass between them. When Posie Parker spoke it was with more than a hint of deliberate coolness.

'Yes. I *do* remember you, as it happens. But I don't recall us ever being the best of pals. Rather the opposite, in fact.'

Posie Parker shoved the chocolate box into her carpet bag haphazardly, and made as if to move off:

'So is this just a happy coincidence or are you following me?'

Felicity forced a smile. 'Both, really. I'm in Cambridge for the same reason as you, I suppose: Dr Rolly's Memorial Service. Poor man, to survive the trenches and then to die of a heart attack in private practice! I wanted to catch you during the luncheon at Trinity College, but you slipped away. So I followed you around town until I could speak to you alone. I read about you in *The Times*. You're a Private Detective now, aren't you?'

Posie Parker nodded. 'Can I help you, Sister Fyne? Otherwise I'll be going. I'm on a pretty tight timetable today.'

'I need you to investigate something for me.'

'Oh?' Posie Parker replied guardedly. 'What?'

'The thing is, and I can't quite believe I'm saying this, to you of all people, but I think I may have seen a ghost.'

'What? Out here?' Posie Parker laughed, rubbing her bare hands together for warmth. 'Dash it all! He must have been hardy! It's freezing!'

Felicity Fyne exhaled slowly and clucked her tongue in visible irritation. She had forgotten that Posie Parker was one of those annoying girls who liked to joke: in fact, she had been famous for it in their unit. That was how a girl with a nice but rather plain face and not-so-trim figure could have befriended most of the men around her; made them act like a bunch of silly overgrown schoolboys. Now Felicity was up close she could see that Posie Parker was wearing a novelty silk scarf underneath her smart coat, printed with a silly motif of garish red reindeers. So much for her new-found sophistication! Had she made a huge mistake in asking for Posie's professional help?

'Frightfully sorry,' Posie Parker said suddenly, her large blue eyes growing deadly serious. 'That was jolly unhelpful of me. I shouldn't joke. It's been a long day. I think I'm in need of a cup of tea. And a cake or two.'

She gestured towards Trinity Street.

'I saw a brand new place which looks good. Will you join me? And then you can tell me all about it.'

* * * *

Of course she remembered her. How could she not?

Posie Parker was queuing up for cakes in Fitzbillies' Tea Rooms, all the while casting surreptitious glances back over her shoulder at Sister Fyne, who was sitting primly at a table set for two in the window, underneath some flickering fairy lights.

'*Once seen, never forgotten,*' or '*The most beautiful girl in the whole wide world.*' Wasn't that what the chaps in their unit used to say about Sister Fyne? Well, that was at first. Later they hadn't been so polite, or forgiving.

Strange, Posie thought, how just as she was here in Cambridge trying to kill two birds already with one stone, yet another phantom from her past should reappear and darken her door. Generally Posie tried to blank out the horrors of the Great War, but it looked as though she'd have to revisit them today.

Posie fingered the silk scarf at her neck, tugging at it. She regretted wearing it now; a silly early Christmas present from her brother's old friend, Lord Rufus Cardigeon. A joke, obviously, but it had also been the only clean thing to hand this morning on the floor of her bedroom which had vaguely matched the colour of her coat. She cursed herself now for offering Sister Fyne tea; she was going to be hampered by limits of time as it was. But something in that lovely face had looked so utterly pained that Posie had found herself almost feeling sorry for the girl. *Almost.* Posie sighed as she handed over the money for the tea things: she'd hear her out, and then politely make her excuses. Sure as bread was bread there'd be a perfectly rational explanation for whatever it was that Sister Fyne *thought* she had seen today.

Posie saw that her companion had now drawn what looked like a small sepia photograph out of her immaculate patent-leather handbag, and she was studying it closely at the table, playing with the folds of the red gingham table-cloth as if for comfort.

Weaving her way back through the crowds of thirsty Christmas shoppers, Posie balanced a large metal tea-pot on a tray with a plate of iced Chelsea buns. A college clock somewhere outside in the darkness was striking five o'clock and a brass band in Trumpington Street struck up a cheery rendition of 'Good King Wenceslas'.

Pouring the tea, Posie found herself unconsciously studying her companion's neck, and then her fingers, but she couldn't immediately think *why*. A vague memory had been disturbed in her mind and was rising uselessly to the surface. But her search for jewellery, if that was it, was fruitless, for Sister Fyne wore nothing but a plain wooden rosary around her neck.

The woman suddenly looked up.

'Do *you* believe in ghosts, Miss Parker?'

'No. I believe there is usually a rational explanation for most things. So, in my book ghosts don't exist,' said Posie resolutely. 'And if they do, I don't care a hang for them.'

'That's what I thought, too. Until today.'

'What's that you've got there?' Posie nodded over at the photo, munching on a bun, keen to avoid all these silly, dramatic turns of phrase. All this talk of ghosts! It was embarrassing for them both. Far better to stick to something certain.

'It's a photo of my husband,' replied Sister Fyne simply, turning the photo this way and that in the twinkling Christmas lights. 'Been dead for almost five years. He died in 1918, at Casualty Clearing Station Number 8, in a direct hit.'

'*What*? A direct hit?' Posie whispered numbly, the news just sinking in. Sister Fyne nodded and continued, barely registering the reaction of her tea-time companion.

'Everyone there died, of course. It was a tragedy.'

Sister Fyne paused:

'Except that I think I saw him today.'

She pushed the photo across the table to Posie. Posie took a sip of her tea to calm herself and then nearly spluttered it all up again over the photo. She hadn't seen that face in a good while, and she hadn't expected to see it again in such strange circumstances.

'Oh, golly,' she whispered. A cold hand clutched at her throat and she felt herself being wrenched back through time against her will. Black tunnels of memories hissed past her like a shrill whistling wind, unwelcoming and cold.

'I had no idea he was dead,' she said softly to Sister Fyne, passing the photo back. 'Or that you actually jolly well went and married him in the end.'

'Of course I married him!' The girl sounded indignant, and half-triumphant. 'Why on earth wouldn't I have?'

Because it was wrong, Posie thought ruefully.

And with a start, she realised that 'it', the whole sorry tale, had happened almost exactly five years before. It had been Christmastime, 1917.

And quite suddenly, she was back there.

* * * *

Two

(Arras, France, 1917)

Ex-policeman Benny Jones took a swig of highly-sugared coffee from his thermos flask and passed it across to Posie, the steam rising in the pearly-grey air. He was a Red Cross medical orderly, and a highly efficient one too. He had just finished checking the knapsack of equipment and supplies their crew kept up front in the ambulance.

Benny broke off a piece of Fry's 'Five Boys' chocolate and ate it quickly for his breakfast. He had a very sweet tooth: he was even worse than Posie.

'Oh rats! This is my last bit of chocolate,' he said in his sing-song Welsh voice. 'I'm hoping me ma will send some more in the post. You live in hope, eh? You got any leave granted over Christmas, Posie?'

Posie shook her head and stroked Merlin, Benny's German Shepherd dog. Merlin was an excellent sniffer-dog and proved invaluable to their crew, finding injured men out on the battlefield every day. A trained police dog in his previous life, he had become a kind of mascot for the crew, too.

'Ah, well. I don't think any of us have been granted any

leave, actually,' Benny said, grabbing a last cigarette and lighting up. 'Apart from Helena.'

He inhaled deeply. 'But no-one can begrudge Helena that. Why, she hadn't been home since the spring! She deserves it, so she does. Her poor old ma will be pleased to see her and give her a nice big hug; a nice big cwtch, as we say in the valleys. Her being an only child, an' all. She's leaving today.'

The two of them plus Merlin were sitting up front in their motor ambulance outside the military mini-hospital, Casualty Clearing Station Number 8, waiting for the night-shift to return, and waiting for the start of their own shift. It was the second week in December. They were watching the sun rise over the frozen fields of Arras, where just five minutes' drive would bring them to the front line of the battle. The engine of their ambulance was running, turning over, keeping itself warm, but you could already hear the steady *dun-dun-dun* of gunfire from the battlefields, and the occasional shell, too. The frozen morning air wafted through the bare window-vents at the sides of the vehicle, where in a normal car glass would have been.

'Helena will be able to share her good news in person with her mother, then, won't she?' said Posie conversationally, trying to stay calm.

Benny nodded, smiling, wiping the steam from his thick glasses with a bit of rag. 'Her ma will be thrilled, I'm sure.'

Posie took a slug of the coffee. 'Not to mention that anything good to come out of this terrible war is worth celebrating. Especially at Christmas.'

They were discussing the very recent engagement of two of Number 8's medical unit; Helena Llewellyn, the nice Welsh Sister-in-charge, and a surgeon, the brilliant Dr Winter, second in command of the unit. An odd match if ever there was one. Nevertheless, the whole unit had celebrated the news of the engagement at an impromptu party the week before.

The fact that Helena was Welsh made Benny fiercely loyal towards her, but she was undeniably a lovely girl, and everyone thought so. Helena was no beauty, but she was the cheerful sort. She was big and capable with brown doe-eyes and raven hair. She was renowned for sharing out her own precious food-parcels with the injured men and for insisting that all the medical staff address her by her first name, which was absolutely unheard of. She also had a rare talent for cake baking, for putting something together out of virtually nothing on the most basic of cooking appliances. She had become justly famous for her ginger cake, which she baked in vast batches on her afternoon off every second week, using the hotel kitchen at the Lion d'Or in Arras by special arrangement with the manager there.

By contrast Dr Winter was horribly aloof, but so handsome and good at his job that although people didn't really like him, he was regarded with respect and something approaching awe by almost all the medical staff. Indeed, it was an undisputed fact that most of the women in the unit could have admitted to having had a schoolgirl crush on Dr Winter at some point during their time there. But not Posie. She had never seen what all the fuss was about, and the haughty Dr Winter had always stayed very much away from her, on the periphery of her existence, which was surprising considering the small team and the cramped working and living conditions.

Posie's fingers shook visibly as she held onto the hot drink, and she tried to tamp down her fear. She had been out on the Western Front for several months now, wanting to be useful, ever since her fiancé, Captain Harry Briskow, had been killed that summer on the Messines Ridge, but if truth were told she was always nervous at the start of a shift. Once she got going it was fine, but the waiting took its toll on the nerves. Just last week an ambulance from the next Clearing Station down from theirs had been totally wiped out by a shell as it returned home, carrying ten wounded soldiers and a complete crew.

Still, there was no point worrying: what could you do but get on with it?

Their medical unit at the Clearing Station was small and tight-knit and they all relied on humour to get through the terrible sights they dealt with every day. There were twenty of them in total, mostly men. In the hospital itself there were two doctors, the Sister-in-charge, a regular Sister, a couple of regular nurses and some male orderlies. There were also the two ambulance crews, and these were made up of a handful of Red Cross volunteers, like herself and Benny Jones.

Her thoughts were broken abruptly by a wild cry from behind them:

'Go! Go! Go!'

Suddenly Bill Wentworth and Harry Smith, two Red Cross stretcher-bearers, came running out of the ramshackle hospital huts, stuffing their breakfast rolls into their mouths and simultaneously pulling on their white regulation armbands emblazoned with a large red cross.

'All right, Posie?' shouted Bill, straightening his tin hat. 'We'd better go. We've spotted our other ambulance heading back this way along the railway tracks, so we'll pass them as we go along. It looked laden down, unfortunately. This way we'll get a head start.'

The two men jumped up easily into the back of the ambulance among the stretchers and medical supplies, and Harry broke into a falsely-cheery rendition of 'If You Were the Only Girl in the World' which they all took up and belted out as loudly as they could.

As they were jolting down the muddy track on the way to the front line, they saw their other ambulance in the distance, returning home, but ahead of it was another grey army truck hurtling its way towards them. Its driver indicated for them to stop, and he leant out of the window, his breath steaming into the frozen air:

'Casualty Clearing Station, Number 8? Nearby, is it?'

Posie nodded and jerked her thumb backwards, her foot very light on the brake pedal, wanting to be off.

'What you got in there, boyo?' asked Benny Jones, leaning across playfully from the passenger seat towards the truck driver. 'I'm *hoping* you're going to tell me it's a load of sweets and letters from home? Post? Or at least replacement medical supplies?'

The driver of the van shook his head:

'Nah, not as such, mate. Replacements though. I'm bringing you a new nurse, and my orders are to take one away.'

If only they had known then just what a portent of doom the truck represented, and just how prophetic the man's words actually were.

* * * *

Sixteen hours later, in the unreliable warmth of the flimsy one-room staff hut, Posie collapsed onto a wooden bench strewn with newspapers and old magazines. Their shift had finished at last.

Wind whipped around the building, promising a storm outside. Her whole body drooped with fatigue. Harry Smith was sleeping already, along with several other staff, all snoring and dozing on the bare floorboards. Next to her, Benny Jones sat down wearily, rubbing his eyes. For once he hadn't got anything to say. It had been a long, long shift and not a particularly happy one either.

Bill Wentworth was frying bacon at the Primus stove in the corner of the hut, feeding Merlin pieces of the fat. Bill had cut big doorsteps of brown bread and had smeared them with butter before laying the bacon on top haphazardly. He came over to Posie and Benny with the sandwiches, placing them on top of an old medical trunk which served as a table.

'Bacon sarnie, anyone?' he said quietly.

As they munched their dinner in inconsolable but companionable silence, the door at the back of the hut was flung open, but not by the wind. Into the dimly-lit room walked an unknown woman carrying a Tilley lamp, straight as a pin, with a face far lovelier than any Posie had seen before. In fact, the woman was breathtakingly beautiful.

Tall and thin with white-blonde hair scraped back off her face into a nursing hood, the woman was pale as a silver Valkyrie. She had huge navy-blue eyes which she blinked very slowly and deliberately. She wore the Sister's official nursing clothes of blue and white, and she looked as cold and proud as the carved figurehead at the mast of a ship. Posie noticed how the men around her suddenly all had their mouths open, slack-jawed. Even Benny and Bill had forgotten about their bacon sandwiches.

'Good evening, volunteers,' said the woman primly, with a pompous manner which Posie immediately hated.

'I am Sister Fyne, Sister Llewellyn's replacement. I'm your new Sister-in-charge for the next three weeks. You will be taking your orders from *me* while you are in this Clearing Station. Do I make myself understood?'

The men were nodding dumbly, but Posie stared at the woman uncomprehendingly. Their small team had been working well enough in this Clearing Station for months now, and yet they were being spoken to by this woman as if *they* had only just arrived, rather than the other way around. And why on earth was the Sister speaking to them as if they were somehow second-rate, just because they were *volunteer* medical workers, rather than people who had had medical careers before the war? The sights they had had to grow accustomed to would make most so-called 'professionals' shudder and recoil in horror.

'What are *you* staring at, nurse?' Sister Fyne snapped at Posie, who continued to chomp on her large sandwich in an unladylike fashion.

'And why are you in here, anyhow? This seems to be the *men's* recreation room. Come here! You should not be in here alone with them. Out! Now!'

Stifling the urge to giggle, and about to point out that there simply *wasn't* anywhere else to go except this one small sparse hut, Benny Jones saved her:

'What about the sixteen hours Posie's just spent, Sister, with only us for company? We was all in one ambulance together; no bigger than this here table we're sitting at now. No chaperone for miles, unless you count the wounded and dying men we were transporting. Nobody had a problem with that then, did they? And she's not a nurse, Sister. She's our ambulance driver, an' all. A proper good one, too.'

But Posie couldn't see or hear what Sister Fyne said in reply, as at that very moment all the lamps and candles blew out.

'Rats! Doesn't make for a good start, does it?' muttered Benny bitterly, as a second quick bang of the door indicated that Sister Fyne had left the hut again. 'Takes herself a touch too seriously, that one, doesn't she? For all her pretty face. Only three weeks to get through though until Helena is back from leave. We'll just have to grin and bear it.'

'Oh, we'll bear it all right,' said Bill Wentworth, laughing. 'Sister Fyne can tuck me into my bed any night she pleases! Coo-ee! What a beauty! Oh, lummie! Don't look at me like that, Benny! And nor you, Posie! You know I'm only joking! Anyway, what can happen in three weeks?'

But fate was not smiling on any of them.

In fact, it seemed a great deal could happen in three weeks.

* * * *

For a start, working conditions quickly got much worse.

In the two weeks leading up to Christmas 1917 the small Clearing Station was simply overwhelmed with casualties. It was harrowing work and the medical staff were all tired. The men needed a distraction in the face of so much death and destruction.

Sister Fyne.

She was in the right place at the right time. Within days of her arrival, the men in the medical unit had fallen under a sort of spell. An infatuation. They began to watch Sister Fyne with rapturous, adoring looks on their faces, whispering in corners about her being '*the most beautiful girl in the whole wide world.*' Posie had never been the jealous type, and she had found it funny at first, but then, as time passed and Sister Fyne's manner towards everybody seemed to get even snappier, even more pompous, Posie found the general adoration by the men simply frightfully annoying. The week before Christmas was especially trying.

One dark, cold afternoon Posie voiced her frustrations about Felicity Fyne to Sister Dulcie Deane, the regular Sister, who was folding lint bandages into neat square bundles in the semi-private sanctity of the supplies cupboard.

Dulcie was the only other half-decent woman in the place, although everyone knew you couldn't trust Dulcie with anything half confidential unless you wanted it spread around the place like wild fire. Dulcie Deane had been transferred to the front line unwillingly, from a big London hospital. Her conversation revolved around just how wonderful her life had been living it up among the bright lights of London, mixed in with any gossip which happened to be going.

'I know it's really trivial,' Posie said, guiltily. 'But it bugs me the way the men can't see through her! When Sister Fyne deigns to speak to you it's as if you're no better than something she's stepped in which niffs a bit! I'm fed up of her.'

Dulcie nodded her head enthusiastically.

'Tell me about it! She has a terribly brusque bedside manner, too. The poor patients! She's never got time to joke or smile for them, either: just keeps muttering on about being 'efficient'. Don't worry about the men in the medical unit. They're a bunch of idiots! I'd like to think the lot of them are hallucinating, as they're so tired; you know, like sailors with mermaids.'

Posie nodded, feeling slightly mollified. She liked the idea of Sister Fyne being likened to a mermaid: it suited her somehow; cold, remote, unreal.

'But I tell you this, it's gone way beyond a joke now.'

Posie started up guiltily from her half-daydream as she realised Dulcie was still chattering away.

'Sorry?'

'I think things might be turning nasty. Guess what I overheard today?'

Posie wasn't really that interested in gossip or in Dulcie's overheard goings-on. She suspected that poor Dulcie was fuelled by a few pangs of jealousy, and who could really blame her? A freckly girl with short dyed-red hair, Dulcie Deane was fairly nondescript, and although she was nice and had always got on with the job in hand, she had so far played a pretty poor second fiddle to the buxom charms of Helena Llewellyn, and she was now paling into absolute insignificance next to the dazzling Felicity Fyne. To her frustration.

'Mnnn? What did you overhear?'

Dulcie frowned, serious.

'Dr Winter is taking Sister Fyne out tonight! Casualties permitting, of course. They've rigged it so they've both got the same evening slot of leave. They're walking out to Arras together. It's a date! Our cool-as-a-cucumber Dr Winter is as silly as the next man for her!'

Posie was brought back to earth with a bump. She didn't really like Dr Winter especially, had never warmed to him or even admired him as the others seemed to, but she wouldn't have expected something as low as *this* from the man. Two-timing.

'*WHAT?*'

Dulcie nodded, her freckled face flashing Posie a look of triumph which only secret knowledge can bring. 'Yes, I heard them talking. They're going to the Lion d'Or for supper.'

Posie frowned, sieving the information for accuracy. It was fairly normal for members of the medical unit to walk to the nearest town, Arras, in their spare time, and sometimes they walked out together or in groups. Two small hotel restaurants on the large town square continued to serve up beer and basic meals to the Allies, despite the destruction in the square itself and in the surrounding cobbled streets, which were all now just heaps of rubble. The biggest hotel, the Lion d'Or, had even allowed the Allied medical staff to come and have a bath there every two weeks, with a strict ticketing arrangement in place. But for Dr Winter and Sister Fyne to go to Arras together, for a meal, *alone*? With no chaperone? It was scandalous, even in wartime. Posie concluded that Dulcie must have got her wires crossed, or misheard. Posie shook her head:

'No, it doesn't signify anything. Maybe it's a professional thing – you've just got the wrong end of the stick, that's all – maybe Dr Rolly's going too?'

'No. He's not. And you don't work in the main ward. *I* do. You should just see the glances passing between the two of them this last week. I don't know where to look sometimes.'

'But what about…'

'Helena?' finished off Dulcie, on a high note. She shrugged rather dramatically. 'Who knows? "*Out of sight, out of mind*", perhaps?'

And so Posie had learnt that it wasn't just the likes of Harry Smith and Bill Wentworth who went gooey whenever Sister Fyne appeared.

Slowly, slowly, the whole unit seemed to learn the truth. That things had moved on to a whole new level, and Sister Fyne was actually *courting* Dr Winter. And then steadily, eventually, the spell was broken. The men in the unit seemed to wake up. Tea-break whispers of '*Is it serious?*' were slowly replaced by '*What about Helena?*' and then, anxiously, '*Is anyone going to tell Helena?*'

An angry, betrayed feeling hung over the unit in the days leading up to Christmas, and Dulcie Deane went around the place with an exaggerated pursed-up mouth, putting up a few pathetic paper chains made from old newspapers in an effort to be festive, and trying to ensure she didn't have to share the same shifts as Sister Fyne.

'It pains me to say it, but *both of them* are to blame,' Benny Jones said miserably on Christmas Eve, as a few medical workers sat cloistered together in the staff hut, smoking and napping between their shifts. Dulcie Deane and Posie were sitting on the floor at Benny's feet, carefully sorting the Christmas goodie tins which had been sent for the injured soldiers by Princess Mary and the Royal Family in England.

'It's Dr Winter's fault just as much as Sister Fyne's, that's what I keep telling myself. I never thought I'd say it but the man's a blaggard. They deserve each other, so they do.'

Dulcie snorted.

'That's as maybe. Anyway, I'll put you all out of your misery and tell you that he's written to Helena at last. Ending it. I saw him today at his little desk in the doctors' ante-room. And then I heard what he said to Sister Fyne.' And here she paused for effect, making sure that everyone in the hut was paying attention.

She continued, relishing the limelight:

'He said: "*Don't worry, I've told her that it's all off. A telegram will go out tonight. We can make things official now. We'll get the Army Chaplain to marry us on his rounds on Boxing Day.*" Make of that what you will.'

Benny Jones tutted to himself sadly. 'Helena will get the telegram tonight, then, in Wales. Rats! What a Christmas present! Poor girl. A broken heart!'

'What will Helena *do*?' asked Bill Wentworth, nervously. 'She's due back here next week. Surely she won't want to work alongside Dr Winter if he's gone and married someone else in the meantime? It would be terrible for her.'

Dulcie Deane sighed. 'She'll have to stay on here, for a while anyway. It takes weeks to organise a transfer for a nursing Sister. The paperwork takes ages. Even in emergencies, even in wartime.'

But as it happened, no paperwork proved necessary.

* * * *

Christmas Day that year was a working day like any other, but a staff Christmas dinner of sorts was organised in two shifts for whoever could attend.

Dinner was set up on a long makeshift trestle-table in the staff hut with old magazine pages laid out haphazardly instead of a tablecloth. People were coming and going in a mad hurry, getting up and down for all the world as if they were playing a real-life game of musical chairs.

It was not a cheerful affair. For once Posie wanted to be alone with her thoughts, not having to pretend to be jolly in a place where there was little to celebrate. To Posie the whole dinner seemed like a strange, surreal blur: half-forgotten pre-war delicacies like roast chicken and crispy potatoes were served up by an army cook, with candied fruits for pudding and extra packets of cigarettes and sweets for whoever wanted them. It felt odd and somehow reckless to be eating Christmas food so close to the front line of a battle.

And Posie felt strangely homesick and lonely, which was unusual. But it was her first Christmas without Harry, for one thing. She missed her brother Richard too. Richard was an Army Officer somewhere out here in the fields of France or Flanders, but *where* he was exactly at the moment was anyone's guess. She was still waiting to hear from him; a letter or a Christmas card, perhaps. But Posie wasn't unduly worried by his silence; she knew that messages between battalions and hospitals even geographically close to each other on the front line could be delayed for days and weeks.

Instead, she had been cheered that morning to receive a small parcel from her father, the Reverend Parker, from his Norfolk Rectory: a bright hand-painted Christmas card of a ruby-red poinsettia, a bottle of her favourite parma violet perfume and a small packet of humbugs from the village shop. Right now her thoughts were dreamily wandering back home to gentle Norfolk: to the green fields unbroken by trenches and barbed wire fences; to the sweep of peaceful golden beaches unspoilt by mines; to the arc of endless blue sky which had formed the backdrop to her childhood. To the blissful silence…

'Penny for your thoughts, Parker?'

Posie looked up from her meal in surprise and saw that the vacant seat opposite her own had been taken by the odious Dr Winter, whom she had only ever spoken to once or twice before, never having much need to spend time in the main ward or operating theatre. He had already started to eat his dinner. The two seats on either side of him were still empty, probably on purpose. The ill-will towards the man was palpable in the room, as if he was emitting a particularly bad stink. Posie sighed and rustled up her manners. It was Christmas, after all.

'I'm sorry, sir. I was miles away. If you really want to know, I was thinking of home.'

He smiled. Dr William Winter was one of those very

tall, nervy, angular men who had been blessed from boy-hood with a fair, sculpted beauty which he carried carelessly but certainly. He was extraordinarily good-looking, and what Posie assumed *The Lady* and other such magazines meant when they described someone as 'easy on the eye'. And he knew it, too. But up close there was something about him which Posie didn't like and which she couldn't quite put her finger on. Something almost reptilian maybe. Perhaps it was the slow, measured blink of the eyes, which were small and sad, or the smile playing needlessly around the mouth, which made him look as if he were enjoying a private joke.

She suppressed a shudder. She noticed how the other staff at the table busied themselves in talking to each other in a frenzy, turning their faces away from Dr Winter, leaving Posie quite alone.

'This your first Christmas at the front, Parker?'

She nodded glumly.

'Chin up, then. It's likely to be your one and only, and *my* last. You'll be back home this time next year, having Christmas in the normal way. We'll have won this bally war by then, just you see, and we'll all be back doing what we were doing before.'

'You'll be back in Cambridge then, sir?'

Dr Winter nodded, spooning tinned mushroom soup into his mouth as quickly as he could. His brilliant career as a surgeon at Addenbrooke's Hospital on Trumpington Street in Cambridge and on Harley Street in London was legendary. It had been cut short when he had volunteered to come out to serve on the front line.

'Do you know Cambridge at all, Parker?'

Posie shrugged. 'Just a little. My brother Richard is a Fellow at Trinity College. Well, he *was*; before the war. He's an Officer out here just now. I suppose he'll go back afterwards. I used to visit him there sometimes.'

'Trinity, eh?' Dr Winter was eating his meal at breakneck speed, checking his wristwatch constantly, needing to get back to his patients. 'I was a Queens' man myself. But you know Trinity is Dr Rolly's college, too, don't you? He's a Fellow there as well. Perhaps they know each other?'

Just at that moment Sister Fyne came into the hut and sat down wordlessly at Dr Winter's right-hand side, marking her territory. Dr Winter turned and smiled quickly at Sister Fyne, a quick sparkling smile filled with absolute happiness which made words quite unnecessary. Sister Fyne picked up her cutlery impatiently and indicated to the cook to come and serve her with a brisk wave of the hand. She stared at Posie angrily with her great navy eyes and Posie looked back down at her almost empty plate, feeling like a third-rate gooseberry, feeling guilty for having even *spoken* to Dr Winter.

How different Sister Fyne was from Helena Llewellyn, Posie reflected. In fact, Dr Winter couldn't have chosen two more different women if he had tried; they were like chalk and cheese. There was no accounting for it: perhaps working here under such dreadful conditions had turned him slightly loopy, and he should be pitied, not hated.

It was then that Posie noticed that everyone else at the table was staring at Sister Fyne as if hypnotised, and suddenly it was hard not to see why: a white, flashing stone was glittering fabulously around Sister Fyne's neck.

Jewellery was not permitted in the Casualty Clearing Station, and any wedding or engagement rings were only allowed if they were worn on a necklace, hidden from view, in line with Red Cross rules. But although this solitaire diamond engagement ring was hung, regulation-like, on a chain, it was certainly not hidden. It was anything *but*. It was being deliberately flaunted. It was a statement of possession. Of achievement.

The diamond seemed to catch all the weak yellow afternoon light in the hut and reflect it back outwards. Posie gasped. Where on earth had Dr Winter got that rock of a ring from? Surely such a beauty couldn't be found in the poor depleted little shops of Arras?

Into Posie's mind came back a sudden remembrance. Helena Llewellyn, just a month before, laughing over a glass of what passed for wine at her so-called 'engagement party', her eyes twinkling, her ring finger with its small round pearl set in a thin band of silver extended out to Posie and Dulcie for their inspection:

'*It's only a poor little thing, but it does the job, doesn't it? William got it in town. At any rate, I'm not fussed about jewels, and just as well, eh? Where would William get a proper engagement ring from now, anyhow? There's a war on and no mistake!*'

Posie was brought back to the present by Benny Jones' sing-song voice.

'My! What a lovely necklace you have on there, Sister Fyne! Must signify something special, does it? Do tell us. We're dying to know. A whopper like that, an' all…'

Everyone at the table went deathly quiet. Posie watched Sister Fyne turn scarlet, then grow white. Dr Winter had the good grace to flush red with embarrassment beside her, averting his eyes from the rest of the table, making a show of grabbing up his black leather medical bag and his white coat behind him, as if to leave.

It was unthinkable! Benny had behaved entirely inappropriately. He was out of order, and in a military hospital such as theirs order and seniority were everything. He had just broken every rule in the book. Why, Benny could face imprisonment for speaking out like that! But just as Sister Fyne was about to open her mouth and respond, a military post-boy entered the hut, looking around nervously.

'Hallo! Merry Christmas to you all! I say, is Dr Winter here?'

Dr Winter waved him over, keen for the distraction.

'The other doctor told me to come in here. It's a telegram for you, sir. Here you go! It's marked "urgent".'

Dr Winter ripped open the telegram and read the contents. All of a sudden there was a kind of groan and the telegram fluttered to the floor.

Everyone at the table stared as Sister Fyne, galvanised into action, simply flew at him, panicking, flapping in a thoroughly uncharacteristic manner like an angry dark crow.

'William! William! What is it? What's happened? Someone you know in London? A Zeppelin raid?'

But Dr Winter just turned to her with an odd blazing gleam in his pale blue eyes. He retrieved the telegram from the floor with shaking hands and rose from the Christmas dinner table uncertainly, like a man caught out unexpectedly in a harsh snowstorm. Ignoring Sister Fyne's protestations, and ignoring her in general, he pushed his way on out of the hut.

Everyone watched, mesmerised, as he loped past the windows of the little staff hut, on his way back to relieve Dr Rolly of his duties, leaving his current fiancée standing alone, looking foolish and uncertain.

There was one question on everyone's lips.

What on earth had been in that telegram?

* * * *

They learnt later on that day what had happened. Or rather, unsurprisingly, Dulcie Deane did.

The telegram was from Helena Llewellyn's mother in Wales. She had written to inform Dr Winter that her only daughter, his fiancée, had been killed the day before, on Christmas Eve.

Helena had apparently decided to return to work early, to surprise Dr Winter by returning in time for Christmas, and the War Office had managed to find her a last-minute passage back to France on a cargo vessel, the *SS Victoria*.

It had been sunk by a German U-boat in the English Channel, with all hands lost.

Mrs Llewellyn had been informed by the War Office as Helena's next-of-kin, but she had immediately telegrammed to Dr Winter, a man she had never met, but whom she felt had an equal right to know.

Posie's crew were on the night-shift, and just before they left for duty, the evening post brought 'official' confirmation of the news; a pink letter from the War Office informing Casualty Clearing Station Number 8 of the death of Sister Llewellyn, and of the permanent appointment of Sister Fyne in her place. Dr Rolly pinned it up on the staff noticeboard, his mouth set in a grim line, before heading back to his patients.

Benny Jones, smoking one cigarette after another, was more upset than he liked to admit.

'Small mercy, but at least she went to her grave still feeling loved,' he said gloomily, checking his torch and fiddling with the Red Cross flag he carried when he went out into no-man's land.

'At least she hadn't had a chance to receive that scoundrel's telegram in which he dumped her!'

'That's very true.' Posie nodded, buttoning up her thick oilskin coat against the freezing night air. 'But my gosh, imagine how Helena's mother must be feeling now, eh? Sure as bread is bread she received that telegram from Dr Winter only a few hours after the one from the War Office. I'm sure she would have read it, even if it had been marked for Helena. She'll be wanting Dr Winter's guts for garters now! And frankly, who can blame her? I wouldn't want to be in his shoes if ever she gets hold of him!'

'Fate will catch up with them both, that's all I can say,' Benny said darkly. 'That telegram about Helena's death will change Dr Winter's life for ever. Not a great start to a marriage, is it? *If* they decide to go ahead with it, I mean.'

And as they headed out into the stormy night, they were blissfully unaware that *their* lives, too, were about to change for ever.

* * * *

Posie was woken the next day by someone calling out her name.

At first she thought she was still dreaming and she hunkered down further inside her sleeping bag. But the voice was insistent, and somehow, somewhere in the back of her mind she recognised it as being important.

'I'm coming!' she yelped blearily. She guessed it was lunchtime. Her tent was freezing, but then it always was, and a low yellow winter sun was shining through the white canvas. She had slept in her oilcloth coat, and underneath it she wore almost all the clothes she had brought with her to France. She pushed her feet into her brown regulation boots and grabbed her wristwatch, and broke the ice on the small tin of water she kept in the corner for washing her face.

'Just coming!'

She emerged from her tent into dazzling bright sunshine, shielding her eyes. The other staff tents seemed totally empty, their entrances flapping loosely in the cold air like a row of white flags. A brilliant blue winter sky blazed overhead.

'Miss Parker?'

A military post-boy stood silhouetted to one side, his foot scrabbling in embarrassment at the scrubby, icy earth.

'Telegram for you, Miss.'

He shrugged apologetically, and passed over the card.

'Sorry to wake you. I was told you had been on night-duty, but it says "urgent" and instructions are to deliver it to the recipient in person, or not at all.'

A strange calm descended on Posie as the post-boy headed off again. The instructions given to the post-boy meant it was news of the very worst sort. Her heart was in her mouth and the hospital huts and the wretched little camping tents all formed a hazy blur around her.

She had been here before: she had received the official 'Deeply regret to inform you…' telegram before, when Harry had died in June. This was somehow similar, and at once Posie knew that she would never forget this Christmas, and for all the wrong reasons.

She ripped the paper open and sank numbly back down into the open mouth of her tent. The telegram read:

MISS PARKER,

NORBERT CARPENTER HERE - YOUR FATHER'S CHAPLAIN. IT IS WITH REAL SORROW THAT I SEND THIS TELEGRAM, FOR IT BRINGS BAD NEWS.

YOUR BROTHER RICHARD DIED AT THE BATTLE OF CAMBRAI IN NOVEMBER. IT SEEMS YOUR FATHER RECEIVED WORD AT THE TIME THAT RICHARD WAS MISSING IN ACTION AND HOPED AGAINST HOPE THAT HE WOULD TURN UP AS A PRISONER OF WAR, OR AS A CASUALTY.

BUT HE HEARD YESTERDAY (CHRISTMAS EVE) FROM AN ARMY CHAPLAIN WHO SERVED ALONGSIDE YOUR BROTHER. HE CONFIRMED RICHARD'S DEATH. THE ARMY CHAPLAIN HAS BEEN UNCONSCIOUS THIS LAST MONTH IN HOSPITAL AND REMAINS VERY ILL, AND ONLY JUST MANAGED TO WRITE A FEW BRIEF

WORDS TO YOUR POOR FATHER.

PLEASE ACCEPT MY CONDOLENCES. I MET RICHARD ONCE OR TWICE AND HE ALWAYS IMPRESSED ME WITH HIS CHEERY COUNTENANCE AND SENSE OF HUMOUR.

THE POINT IS - AND IT IS RATHER AWKWARD - YOUR FATHER HAS NOT GOT OUT OF BED SINCE HEARING THE NEWS. I CANNOT BRING HIM ANY COMFORT AND I AM DEEPLY FEARFUL FOR HIS HEALTH, BOTH BODY AND SOUL.

AS THE ONLY FAMILY HE NOW HAS, I WONDER, CAN YOU ARRANGE IT SO YOU CAN COME HOME AND TEND TO YOUR FATHER AS A MATTER OF SOME URGENCY?

AGAIN WITH DEEPEST SYMPATHIES.

I REMAIN, YOUR HUMBLE SERVANT,

THE REV. N. CARPENTER

And without thinking, Posie found herself automatically packing her knapsack, tidying her little tent and taking off her Red Cross armband and the Red Cross pin which she had worn with such pride for five months.

She would go and report to Dr Rolly as the head of the Casualty Clearing Station, tell him she was leaving, and then inform the Red Cross who officially employed her. But it was a mere formality. She couldn't stay on here: she would leave today.

She was going back home. But Richard, her lovely brother, would not be there. He would never be there again. The smarting realisation of what the telegram *really* meant was beginning to hit home: tears were pricking at her eyes.

Random memories of her elder brother suddenly and inconveniently crammed themselves into her mind, all out of order and higgledy-piggledy: Richard as a boy, climbing trees in the Rectory gardens; Richard whizzing down the stair-bannisters of the house at breakneck speed in the school holidays, daring Posie to join him, and then, one summer not so long gone, when he had already been appointed a Fellow at Cambridge and was back home for a few weeks on leave, Richard mooning around the house for days on end. Uncharacteristically sad.

Oh, Richard, Posie wanted to scream aloud. *Couldn't you have managed to stay alive? For me?*

But all she was really left with was a nagging emptiness.

Anger at her father bubbled up, too. Why on earth hadn't her father told her about the telegram which must have arrived in November, telling him that Richard was missing in action? Was it really a sort of naivety which she could well imagine her father capable of? Or had he wanted to shield Posie from what could have been an awful truth for as long as possible?

Her heart fluttering with a sadness and a heaviness she hadn't felt in a long time, she crossed over to the staff hut to say goodbye forever to her crew. She fought back the tears which she knew would come, but which she would save for later, when she could grieve in private.

* * * *

Posie had spent the rest of the war cocooned in the Norfolk Vicarage, where, apart from a couple of mad weeks around the time of the Armistice when she had helped the Red Cross out as an ambulance driver yet again, she had calmly and efficiently taken over the running of the Rectory and nursed her father out of his collapse, although it was fair to say he was never the same man again.

And within days of returning home to Norfolk those crazy, gut-wrenchingly tiring days she had spent working on the front line seemed like years ago. Another lifetime ago.

She was forced to grieve in private for her brother Richard, and for Harry Briskow, and for other friends who had fallen. She didn't dare mention her brother in general conversation in case it brought on another attack of her father's nerves.

Posie had been at home for about a month when she heard from Dulcie Deane, whom she hadn't had time to keep in touch with, with some news out of the blue.

A few short lines in a distinctive hand arrived on the back of an army regulation postcard:

Posie,

Thought you might want to know, your old ambulance crew were all killed last week. Blown up by a mine. Including the dog.

Seems that you had a lucky escape.

Here at Clearing Station Number 8 all else remains the same.

Best regards,
DULCIE

P.S. Look me up in London when this is all over at my hostel, W1 D. Would be nice to keep in touch.

And so it was that Posie had learnt that they were all dead; Benny Jones and Merlin, and Harry and Bill. And all she could do was to add them to the list of those she grieved for. She tried not to dwell on whether or not she had had a lucky escape, and focused instead on just living.

And her life had proven busy, but underneath it all a sadness lingered.

Like a bad cut which would not heal.

* * * *

Three

(Cambridge, 1922)

'So Clearing Station Number 8 took a direct hit, did it? *When* was that exactly, Sister Fyne?'

Posie was trying to be business-like, trying to forget her personal connection with the place. But it was hard. Her thoughts were still in Arras, back in 1917…

'February, 1918. And call me Felicity, please. We don't need to be so formal now, do we?'

Posie shrugged as if the familiarity meant little to her. 'You'd better call me Posie then.'

Posie chewed her lip half-guiltily and uncapped her pen, arranging her notebook in front of her. She hadn't been informed of the loss of the Clearing Station before, not having stayed in touch with anyone left there after her crew had died, and it felt both sad and odd to hear about it now. She felt a twinge of remorse for poor dead Dulcie Deane whom she hadn't written back to; remorse for all those tireless Red Cross workers and medical staff, and pity too for the poor soldiers who had been brought to a place of supposed safety and healing. She surprised herself by even feeling a stab of sadness at the death of fickle, aloof Dr Winter.

'Forgive me for asking, Felicity, but how come *you* survived to tell the tale?'

'I was the only one. I'd been working solid shifts for two weeks running and I was due an afternoon's leave.'

Felicity Fyne paused and held the edges of her handbag tightly, as if keeping herself moored to one place. Even in the frenzied jumping of the blue and green fairy lights, she was still so beautiful that it quite took your breath away. Her harsh, well-cut black clothes and old-fashioned hairstyle only served to display her remarkable looks all the more. She looked like a glamorous nun. Felicity took a deep shuddering breath and went on:

'It was Valentine's Day. Ridiculous, I know. But I had decided to walk to Arras and buy some lace for myself, and some bits and pieces for William – Dr Winter – as well. It was unseasonably good weather, almost warm in fact, and I lingered on the walk back. I remember I even picked some early daffodils on the way – they seemed so cheerful and at odds with all the bloodshed – and when I got back, there was nothing left. The Clearing Station had been bombed.'

As Felicity Fyne spoke, a single tear rolled down her pale, unmade-up face.

'There was just this huge crater in the ground where the staff hut and the ward hut used to be, and everyone was dead. It was horrendous.'

'So no chance of any survivors? Dr Winter couldn't have escaped somehow and done a bunk?'

Posie was thinking about how the war had offered endless chances for people to disappear, to reinvent themselves, to find a new life; to live double lives. And nothing could be proved. Especially after the mess caused by large-scale destruction. She'd never dealt with such a case herself, but she was aware of the possibilities.

Felicity Fyne shook her head. 'No way. Not a chance. Everyone died that day. Staff and patients.'

Posie was busy scribbling. Felicity Fyne continued, staring at the photograph on the table between them.

'There's another thing, though, if you're after "proof". Naturally it was *I* who was asked to go through William's personal things, and I swear everything important was left there in his tent: this photograph, his identity card, his passport, his ration book, a crummy old copy of a Shakespeare play, his medical practice certificates, our marriage certificate, even though we'd only been married six weeks at that point. So there's your proof!'

'How so?'

'I needed most of those documents when I applied to the War Office to claim my War Widow's Pension. And there's no way that if William had somehow survived that blast he could have run away *without* those documents. He wouldn't have got far. Certainly not all the way home. He would have been brought back again. Or Court Marshalled instead, for cowardice.'

Posie changed tack, feeling her way: 'But you think you saw him today?'

Felicity Fyne nodded. 'Yes. Just for a moment. At the very back of Trinity College Chapel. Near the marble carvings and memorials. I went cold all over. It gives me goose bumps just talking about it now, even. He was loitering there, leaning against the last pew, and I swear that when he saw me he turned quickly and walked out.'

'What made you think it was him? It was fairly dark today, especially in the Chapel. It could have been anyone, surely?'

'No.' Felicity Fyne looked Posie straight in the eye. 'Don't you remember his height, his way of standing? It was definitely him, or a twin brother, if he had had one, which he didn't. Or, as I said, his ghost.'

'I told you. Ghosts don't exist.' Posie frowned. 'Was there anything special about him today, or different, maybe? Anything especially noteworthy?'

'No. Oh! Oh, yes! Wait a minute... There *was* one strange thing. He was wearing a university gown. And he looked sort of dusty. Shabby really. He was always so very smart before, even during emergencies on the wards. Impeccably turned out. So *that* was odd.'

Posie noted this all down in her notebook, privately surprised at how scanty the details were and trying not to look at her wristwatch for the time.

'Did your husband have any other family at home? Anyone you've been in touch with?'

Felicity shook her head. 'He was an only child of only children. His parents lived in Glasgow before the war. His father was a bigwig surgeon up there at the Royal Infirmary. Famous, apparently. William followed him into medicine; I gather it was a family tradition. The father was a really cold fish, though. He didn't want to know me when I wrote to him asking if we could meet following William's death. He sent me a short note basically telling me to bog off. Very unfriendly.'

'And the mother? Were you in touch with her at all?'

Felicity shook her head. 'No, I never heard from her at all. Although I addressed my letter to both of them.'

Posie nodded and took a few other personal details such as Dr Winter's date of birth and height and eye colour, and then she asked her routine final question: one she always asked clients, whether or not she took the case on.

'And is there anything else important which comes to mind?'

Felicity Fyne shook her head, but just for a second Posie saw what looked like a flutter of fear, or a smidgen of embarrassment pass over her features.

'You're *sure* there's nothing else you want to tell me?'

'No, nothing. So what do you make of it all, Posie?'

Posie looked up into Felicity Fyne's hopeful face. Personally she thought it was a mare's nest and that the woman was being delusional, and that her short, heady marriage to Dr Winter had turned him into some sort of saint in her memory. This was evidenced by the fact that Felicity still wore old-fashioned black mourning clothes almost five years after his death, and clutched at a photograph of the man as if he had just died yesterday. Felicity Fyne couldn't, or wouldn't, move on. Posie put down her pen and pad and splayed her hands apologetically.

'Honestly, I think I'm going to find out very little. It sounds implausible to me. Perhaps it was a trick of the light in the Chapel? Or a lookalike? Unless of course Dr Winter was, by some miracle, hurt rather than killed at the time of the bombing in 1918 and disappeared for some private reason of his own. But then why on earth would he decide to come back today to Cambridge and honour his former colleague, Dr Rolly? Why would he be so *stupid*? To risk being found out in such a blatant way; in a place where he had a high chance of being recognised?'

A flicker of anticipation flashed across Felicity Fyne's face. Posie cut in quickly, sensing her mistake in allowing false hopes to take root.

'But I don't believe that theory for one minute. I have to tell you, Felicity, that I get a lot of cases of women coming to me, asking me to investigate their missing menfolk from the war. Mainly it's women whose men went missing in action, so there's no grave for them to grieve at. They continue to hope and pray that by some miracle their men will still turn up, all these years later, perhaps having been injured or having developed amnesia or something.'

'And? Have you had any successes with those cases? There must be *some* good news?'

Posie made an expressive grimace. 'Actually, I've simply never taken on one of those cases. I listen sympathetically and then I turn the women away. The truth hurt the first time around when they got those dreadful telegrams. I don't want to be the bearer of the same awful truth a second time over. Besides which, they'd be paying to hear me spell out the sad old news all over again. I can't justify it and I jolly well won't do it. They're hopeless cases.'

'So what you're saying, politely, is that you've listened to me tell my story, and now you won't take it? It's – as you call it – a hopeless case?'

'Yep. I'm afraid so. It wouldn't be fair. To you. Or to your purse.'

Felicity Fyne seemed to hesitate, and then she pulled out something else from her black patent-leather handbag. It was a regular-sized white envelope, stamped and addressed and post-marked from London. It looked a little worn at the corners, as if it had been carried around quite a bit.

'This might make you change your mind,' Felicity Fyne said softly. 'I haven't been entirely honest with you. I believe I saw William today, or whatever it was that looked like him, but I probably wouldn't have followed you, or tried to obtain your help if it hadn't been for *this*.'

She gingerly pushed the envelope across the table. 'You see, the idea about William still being alive has been very much in my mind lately. Someone else thinks so, too. And wanted me to know about it. I received *this* last week.'

Posie took the envelope deftly and drew out a plain, cheaply-printed Christmas card of a group of carol singers, the sort you could buy at any London Underground stationery booth. A sliver of cheap green glitter came off on her fingertips as she opened the card.

Posie read the written message inside:

DECEMBER 1922,

MISS FYNE,

YOUR HUSBAND IS ALIVE AND WELL. (AS I'VE TOLD YOU TWICE BEFORE BUT WHICH YOU'VE CHOSEN TO IGNORE.)

IF YOU WANT MORE INFORMATION ON HIS WHEREABOUTS IT WILL COST YOU DEARLY,

ALTHOUGH IT WOULD HAVE BEEN MUCH CHEAPER IF YOU HAD RESPONDED WHEN I FIRST WROTE TO YOU IN 1920.

TO INDICATE YOU WISH TO OBTAIN THIS INFORMATION PLEASE FILL YOUR WINDOW WITH RED HATS ON CHRISTMAS EVE THIS YEAR. I WILL THEN TELL YOU HOW TO PROCEED AND HOW TO GET THE MONEY TO ME.

IF I DO NOT SEE THE RED HATS ON DISPLAY THIS YEAR I WILL NOT COMMUNICATE WITH YOU AGAIN.

HOWEVER, I WILL REPORT YOU TO THE RELEVANT AUTHORITIES AND SEE THAT ALL NECESSARY MEASURES ARE TAKEN AGAINST YOU. IN IGNORING THIS INFORMATION, YOU ARE COMMITTING A CRIMINAL FRAUD. AS YOU WELL KNOW.

MERRY CHRISTMAS.

Posie looked up, gobsmacked:

'Let me get this right. You're being blackmailed? And this is the *third* communication you've received from this person?'

Felicity Fyne nodded dismally. 'Yes. It's the third Christmas in a row I've received the very same card.'

Posie whistled softly. 'My gosh! This certainly puts a different spin on things.'

She picked up her pen again and re-read the Christmas card thoughtfully.

'There's so much here I don't understand. But,' Posie added after a moment, 'I can only help you if you're willing to fill me in on the background. There's no use if I only know half the story. Are you willing to answer my questions truthfully this time?'

Felicity Fyne nodded and murmured, 'Yes. I'm sorry I

didn't show you this before. In truth I was ashamed, I didn't know what to do. And I was scared. I was approaching Christmas with a sense of dread, knowing I would probably receive this, but hoping that the writer would simply give up this year. I didn't believe them, either. I thought it was all a hoax. Until today, that is.'

'So you've no idea who the writer of the cards is, then?'

Felicity Fyne shook her head quickly. 'No. It could be anyone. I worked in several hospitals before I came out to Arras, and then I worked at several more Clearing Stations after Number 8 was bombed, up until the war ended. I always rubbed people up the wrong way somehow. It could be *anyone* who bears me a grudge.'

'How much does the blackmailer want? There's no price mentioned here.'

Felicity Fyne sighed. 'Thirty pounds. That was two years ago, and it says they want more now.'

Posie inhaled sharply: it seemed an awful lot to ask for. 'I hope you don't mind my asking, but can you afford that? It seems such a great deal of money. As if they believe you do *have* spare money to hand over.'

'No.' Felicity Fyne shook her head certainly. 'I can't afford it in a million years.'

Posie nodded, jotting things down, underlining some of them. She looked up again and went on:

'"*Red hats*"? Does that make any sense to you?'

Felicity Fyne nodded and took a small silver card-holder from her handbag. Out of it she took a neat cream business card, and passed it to Posie, who read it quickly:

VERY FYNE HATS.
FOR ALL YOUR MILLINERY NEEDS.
Address: 2, The Parade, Hampstead Heath,
London, NW3.
Proprietor: Mrs Felicity Winter-Fyne.

'Ah!' Realisation dawned on Posie, mixed with real surprise. Felicity Fyne had always been so adamant at pointing out to people that she was a *professional* nurse, rather than a lowly volunteer, and had seemed very proud of her chosen profession.

'I see. Sorry, I assumed you were still a nursing Sister. So you own a hat shop now?'

'Correct. I own the shop and design all the hats I sell. I gave up nursing when the war finished. I couldn't bear it any more. I had seen too much. I wanted a new start, and I've always loved fashion, and hats especially. I felt like doing something frivolous. I sold everything I had, and I started the shop up in Hampstead. It's early days, of course, but it's not doing too badly. But it's certainly not making enough money for me to squander away thirty pounds on information which may or may not prove to be accurate.'

Posie nodded, more and more surprised by Felicity Fyne. An image of a surreal hat shop, very like a hospital ward, all starchy and steel-panelled, came uncalled for into Posie's mind. She shrugged it off quickly. She waved her pen in the air, business-like.

'Last question, I promise.'

'Fire away.'

'Do you know what the writer means in this last part? Saying they will "report you to the relevant authorities"? What fraud are they on about?'

Again Felicity Fyne nodded, and smiled ruefully.

'I presume the writer means to report me for drawing a War Widow's Pension each month. It's quite a substantial amount, you know. And *if* William is alive, obviously I have no right to it. Not to mention that I would have to pay it back, all five years' worth. A tidy sum. And one I can't afford. To be honest it's the pension which has kept the hat shop afloat these last few years really, allowed me to pay for fabrics and a couple of local seamstresses. There's only so many of your own things you can sell. I don't have anything valuable left.'

Instinctively Felicity's hands flew to her neck.

That was it! The memory broke through into the here and now and Posie spoke without caution.

'Your engagement ring from Dr Winter, you mean? That huge diamond you wore on a chain? You sold it?'

Felicity nodded.

'Yes. That's right. It *was* my engagement ring, but it was my grandmother's ring first, actually. It was an heirloom. William didn't buy it for me, if that's what you're getting at. I had it with me in my knapsack when I was sent out to the front line. I always had it with me; it was my good luck charm. It seemed silly for William to run off and buy another ring when he proposed; I had this perfectly good one with me already. Anyway, where would William have got a diamond engagement ring like that from? There was a war on!'

Posie raised her eyebrows. She remembered the resentment the ring had caused when Felicity had worn it so proudly, and Benny Jones' stinging attack. How wrong they had all been! It seemed appearances could be very deceptive.

'You're thinking about that horrible Christmas dinner, aren't you?' said Felicity, softly. 'When I wore the ring out in public?'

Posie nodded uncertainly.

'You didn't help yourself much there. You put people's backs up. We all thought Dr Winter had bought you the ring and you were showing off. It just made an awkward situation worse, somehow.'

'I know. I wanted to celebrate – it was Christmas after all – and I thought it would be an instant way to show people we were engaged, without having to make big explanations. Especially after William's broken engagement with that fat girl. But I knew it was wrong the moment I sat down and everyone stared at me with real hatred in their eyes. I was burning up inside, but I couldn't rip the thing off, could I? I just had to get on with it as best I could and sit it out.'

Posie was surprised at the girl's frankness, and said so.

Felicity shrugged:

'What do I have to lose in telling you all this now, anyhow? I wish I hadn't worn it, but what's done is done. Besides, everyone who was sitting at that dinner table in 1917 except you and me are now dead, and beyond caring. Anyway, I didn't give a hang about any of those people there that day. They were all wretched bores.'

That included me! Posie thought wryly, trying to keep a straight face and not let her personal feelings enter the equation. *I was just another wretched bore.*

She reflected how Felicity Fyne, no matter how altered by the making of hats rather than the fixing of bodies, had an unfortunate manner. She was still arrogant and strange. In fact, there was something detached about her; as if she was looking at the world and everybody in it through the thick glass lens of a camera. Try as she might Posie couldn't begin to feel even slightly sorry for her.

She looked up and saw Felicity Fyne's eyes burning intensely across the table at her, filled with desperation.

'So what do you think?'

Posie realised that she still disliked Felicity Fyne, but if there was one thing Posie really couldn't stand it was a blackmailer, particularly one who could get people's hopes up in this awfully cruel way: it seemed almost one hundred percent certain to Posie that Dr Winter was dead and buried.

'I'll take the case,' Posie said quickly, before she could change her mind. She drew out her own business card from her carpet bag and pushed it across the table. 'I'll try and get to the bottom of this for you. I take it you don't want me to involve the police?'

Felicity Fyne shook her head. 'Not if you can help it. No.'

'Tell me, do you want to know the truth about your husband, at any cost? Even if it's not what you really want to hear?'

Felicity nodded her head firmly. 'Yes. He was my everything. But I need to know what's happened.'

'Can I just ask something rather indelicate?' Posie said quickly and quietly. At Felicity's silence she continued:

'I take it you haven't met someone else, since Dr Winter died, I mean? It could make things a bit tricky, that's all, if, for example, you wanted to get married again and we find Dr Winter alive and well. Then obviously a second marriage won't be an option for you.'

Felicity made a moue of distaste:

'Don't you worry on that score. I'll never marry again. Never. I owe it to William. To his memory.'

'But you're…'

'*His*. Still.' Felicity said conclusively, indicating that the subject was not up for further discussion.

Posie had been about to say *beautiful*. What a waste.

'Can I take these?' Posie gestured towards the Christmas card and the photograph of Dr William Winter on the table.

Felicity Fyne nodded and the two women collected their coats and hats and passed out of the tea rooms together onto the cold street outside, Posie jiggering around awkwardly with her many shopping bags, and Felicity Fyne as graceful and unencumbered as a lone swan.

'Oh! Hang on a minute!' said Posie. 'Did you keep the other Christmas cards from the blackmailer?'

Felicity nodded.

'Good. Can you send them to my Grape Street office by the evening post tonight? I'll be back in London tomorrow, and I'll have a look at them then. You never know, they might be useful. I promise I'll visit you in Hampstead before Christmas Eve. That gives me almost a week to find out what I can. Then you can decide how to proceed, with the colours of your shop window display, I mean. Just don't expect too much, though. I'm not that hopeful.'

'Thank you. I know that I can depend on you,' Felicity said quickly, as if in a hurry over her words.

'I saw how others trusted you in the unit. To be honest I was a little jealous of you at times. The men loved you. And I think they loved Helena, my predecessor, too. William never spoke of her to me, and I convinced myself that she wasn't good enough for him, but everyone raved on and on about her. She was *warm*, apparently. Nobody warmed to me. It was my fault, I suppose. I was so concerned with being efficient that I didn't make time for actually getting to know anyone. I think, looking back, that I was nervous. Number 8 was my first post as a Sister-in-charge. I spent the whole time thinking I was about to mess up.'

Posie almost fell off the kerb in surprise, but she stayed silent. She had detested Felicity when she worked with her at the Clearing Station, but it seemed she had misjudged the woman.

Felicity Fyne coughed awkwardly. 'Well, now look at me! Here I am all alone in the world. Some would say it serves me right, I suppose.'

Posie remembered, out of the blue, Benny Jones' dark remark, made long ago, about fate catching up with itself, and she pushed the thought quickly to the back of her mind. She shivered in the late afternoon winter gloom, the bitter cold seeming to invade her very bones. She pulled her cream collar tightly to herself.

Felicity made to leave, then looked directly at Posie and added quickly:

'Forgive the personal question, Posie, but I see you didn't marry? You don't wear a wedding ring on your finger. So you're single, too?'

Posie's face smarted, first at the memory of her dead fiancée Harry and then at the complicated mess which was her current love-life; her relationship with the very famous explorer Alaric Boynton-Dale which had been burning slowly for over a year now but which seemed constantly in danger of fizzling out, due to long absences caused by his travelling. It was a relationship which had so far remained a secret to almost everyone.

Posie shook her head briefly, giving no explanation, hoping to convey the fact that the topic was seriously out-of-bounds. Besides, she had no wish to claim some sort of unmarried solidarity with Felicity Fyne.

'I'm sorry,' said Felicity. 'I'm just surprised, that's all.'

Felicity inclined her head in farewell and walked off down a lamp-lit Trumpington Street in the direction of the Cambridge train station without another word or a backwards wave of the hand.

Posie watched her heading back towards the train to London, a sad black figure in her widows' weeds, disappearing into the endless darkness of the evening; heading back towards her hat shop, and to whatever future Posie might eventually rake up for her.

* * * *

Four

It had started to rain outside. A sleety, heavy, can't-see-where-you're-going sort of rain. Unfortunately Posie hadn't thought to pack an umbrella in among her things for the Memorial Service earlier that day, but she was thankful that she knew where she was going at any rate, as the wet darkness of the December evening seemed to crowd in on you like a suffocating embrace. Posie clutched her paper shopping bags, trying as best she could to stop them from disintegrating.

She turned away in the opposite direction from Felicity Fyne and walked quickly back through the centre of town, her thoughts very much with the woman whom she had just taken tea with. Posie knew Cambridge like the back of her hand. She walked in a world of her own along the dark glistening cobbles of King's Parade, and on past the mass of bicycles tethered together outside the looming darkness of King's College.

Coming up Trinity Street a couple of late shoppers with umbrellas were scurrying along, anxious to get home, but generally not many people were about; term had ended for the university students and most had left to go home for Christmas already.

Posie reached Trinity College, lamp-lit in the darkness,

and swung in under the magnificent carved yellow-stone gatehouse with its little bulbous statue of King Henry the Eighth set high up in the masonry. A prim white sign outside announced *CLOSED TO CASUAL VISITORS*.

The college clock was just chiming six o'clock as she passed through the little wooden gate set into the elaborate stonework of the main gatehouse. Her boots echoed on the yellow-stone flagstones and she saw that she was the only person about. She stopped at the Porter's Lodge which was tucked inside under its own cosy little stone archway. The small office was festively arrayed with bits of holly and silver tinsel and strings of Christmas cards. Behind the wooden-and-glass partition a Porter in his early thirties sat reading an evening edition of a London paper by the bright light of a small lamp.

He was so engrossed in the front page that he didn't see Posie waiting impatiently, anxious to get to her room to dry off before dinner. She craned her neck to see what the main story might be.

'LOVERS WILL HANG!' read the headline.

Posie sighed as she realised it was yet another instalment in the grisly yet horribly sad murder trial which had gripped the nation; the case of Edith Thompson and Freddie Bywaters, the strangely glamorous pair who had both just been found guilty of murdering Edith's husband, Percy, in cold blood. The Porter was obviously ghoulishly revelling in the tragedy, lapping up the details of the verdict.

'I say,' cut in Posie, rapping on the glass divide. 'Are there any telegrams or telephone messages for me? My name is…'

'Miss Rosemary Parker! No need to tell *me*!' announced the Porter, getting to his feet hurriedly and nodding his shiny, round, black-bowler-hatted head in Posie's direction like an old friend. He was very thin and under the hat his ears, which were over-large, stuck out comically. He grinned triumphantly:

'I know you, Miss! I never forget a face! You're the sister of Dr Richard Parker. As *was*, I mean.' Here the Porter doffed his hat momentarily as a mark of respect for the dead before donning it again.

'We was all so sorry to hear of Dr Parker's death in the war; a real nice fellow, he was. None better. I remember you was up here sometimes, with your dad, weren't you, Miss? Lots of times, in fact.'

Posie was stunned. Try as she might she didn't recognise the Porter at all. And she was jolted back in time unwillingly yet again. It was true; she and her father *had* visited Richard countless times over the course of several years. First when Richard had been a science student here at Trinity College, and then, later, when he had been made a Fellow and a lecturer in Botany at the university. He had specialised in the use of plants for medicines, and the scientific use of certain flowers. He had been excited about his work: had hoped to contribute to some big medical breakthroughs in the future.

Looking back to that time before the Great War was like looking through a rose-coloured glass. Posie and her father had frittered away hot afternoons walking together along the River Cam, listening to Richard talk rapturously about his plans for a future which he could not know did not exist for him. They had idled away precious summer days by playing languid games of sloppy tennis at the back of the college. Or sometimes they had punted to Grantchester, taking turns at steering the fragile little wooden gondolas through the sticky bulrushes and taking tea in the Orchard Tea Rooms; napping in green-and-white striped deckchairs and reading novels and newspapers to pass the time. Those long summer days had seemed like they would never end.

Posie swallowed down a lump in her throat. Would they have acted differently if they had known that their time together as a family was to be so short? Would they have acted more seriously? Spoken of more important things?

Probably not.

Posie stared at the big-eared Porter curiously. He had been keeping up a steady flow of chatter as her thoughts had drifted kaleidoscopically over days long gone. He passed her a couple of telegrams solemnly through the cubby-hole of the divide.

'Thank you. But my gosh! How on earth did you recognise me?' Posie blurted out.

She was uncomfortably aware that she had changed, and not just a bit. Before the war she had been slim and rakish, boyish even. She had had long dark hair worn in a thick plait down her back with a big straw boater. Now she was pushing thirty she was better dressed for sure, and had had her hair cut in the fashion of the times, very short, but she was fatter all over. A definite layer of seal blubber was all hers now for the taking.

'The eyes.' The Porter nodded seriously.

'You have the self-same eyes as your brother and I saw him every day, at least once, standing where you are now, Miss, over the course of several years. I knew him out of college too, Miss. We played in the same cricket team on Sundays. Just a pub team, mind. It was the team at the Red Bull. Bit unconventional, I suppose, mixing town and gown, but he was never one for conventions, was he, your brother? He didn't want to play for the university or his Department for some reason, but their loss was our gain: we couldn't have asked for a better bowler, and that's the truth of it. Want to see? I keep a photograph tacked up here of the cricket team before the war, for old times' sake. Looking at you now is like seeing Richard's ghost. Uncanny, it is.'

Ghosts! Posie thought to herself irritably. *What was it with ghosts today? Had everyone gone barmy? Why were they the first thing on everyone's mind?*

The Porter reached up and took down a dog-eared photograph from the wall of his office. He passed it through the divide. And there, among the white-clad team of eleven cricketers, was Richard Parker, nonchalantly leaning on a bat, trying to make himself look shorter, his lopsided grin splitting his handsome face in two. The year was marked in thick white letters at the bottom: '1913'.

'But *you* look happy, Miss,' continued the Porter in a confidential tone, taking the photo back reverently, 'if you don't mind my saying so. Your brother was *not*. He seemed very out of sorts for the last couple of years I knew him here. Haunted, almost. I hope I'm not speaking out of turn, but some of us wondered if everything was quite okay. Do you know what was bothering him?'

Posie looked for a moment into the man's gimlet eyes and realised how very astute he was; how nothing much escaped his notice.

Because it was true.

In the last couple of years before he went off to the war in 1916 something *had* changed; something *had* been wrong with Richard. But Posie was the last person to know what the problem had been. A strange cloud had seemed to hang over her brother which at the time Posie could not understand, which Richard would not *let* her understand. His laughing, dancing eyes had been filled with a distant pain and a sort of strange disbelief. Posie had never got to the bottom of what the problem had been, and it had eaten away at her. It bothered her still. Even though poor Richard had been dead these last five years.

Above all she was here in Cambridge now for Richard. To try and work out what had been bothering him. *Better late than never*, she had reasoned to herself. She had seen the advert in *The Times* for Dr Rolly's Memorial Service, and she had decided to attend. But it was the flimsiest of excuses. Posie had been meaning to come up to Cambridge for ages. For a year, at least.

Ever since she had received a strange letter at Christmas last year. A very odd little letter, in fact.

The Porter was studying Posie with his eagle, well-practised eyes, awaiting some kind of response. Was it her imagination or was there a sort of knowing watchfulness in the Porter's gaze? Did *he* know something useful about her brother?

Posie shrugged non-committally, keen not to share any of her thoughts or fears about Richard.

'I can't say I noticed anything much at all. It's all so much water under the bridge now. Have a good evening, Mr... Mr...? I'm sorry, I don't know your name.'

'Simpkins, Miss. And I'm obliged to you. Have an enjoyable stay at the Master's House tonight, Miss, and a very good trip back to London tomorrow. And an enjoyable dinner this evening, too, at Formal Hall. But take my advice, Miss. You're sitting to the left of Professor Somerjay at the High Table. Once he gets talking you'll be stuck with him all night, there's no escaping him. Better by far to start as you mean to go on; on your left will be Dr Greenwood. He was connected to your brother, in the Botany Department. Talk to him. I think you'll learn much.'

Posie almost gasped. That the Porter knew her whole itinerary, not to mention her place at dinner was staggering. Almost uncanny. Simpkins laughed, reading her mind:

'That's what we're paid to do, Miss, in this job. *Observe.* Gather information. Even in a college with more than five hundred students I can still tell if anyone from outside is sneaking in for a free dinner. That's what we're trained to do – spot outsiders – and not much gets past me, I can tell you. Photographic memory for faces,' he tapped his head proudly with two stubby fingers, 'that's what I've got here. Not much gets past old Stan Simpkins.'

Posie started at the mention of the photographic memory. It was an odd way to approach things, certainly, but then, it had been an odd sort of day, and it was a dashed strange sort of a problem...

She dived into her carpet bag, dislodging her box of

chocolates as she went. She grabbed them precariously and found the photograph of Dr Winter which Felicity Fyne had given her not one hour previously. She pushed it through the glass divide.

'I say, it would be jolly amazing if you could help me out with this one, Simpkins. I could do with your photographic memory here.'

Simpkins had picked up the photograph and was studying it intently. He looked longingly at the box of chocolates still clutched in Posie's hand. Quick as a flash she had pushed them through the divide too.

'These are for you, Simpkins. I need you to tell me if you saw this man today. Around lunchtime. He was a possible attendee at Dr Rolly's Memorial Service. Take your time. Much is riding on it. I'm expecting a negative response by the way; it's most likely he *wasn't* here today. So don't be ashamed to say if you didn't see the man.'

Simpkins looked crushed. 'I'm so very sorry, Miss. I can't help you, more's the pity. I only came on duty this evening.' He started to push the chocolates back through the divide, then thought better of it.

'But I tell you what. My colleague Frank Bevans was on duty at lunchtime. He'll have noticed this fella come through the gates. Never misses a trick, old Frank, like me. Loves the job too, like I do. I know where to find him this evening. I'll ask him just as soon as I finish my shift in a minute and I'll let you know what he says first thing tomorrow morning. I'll come in specially.'

A gaggle of very wet, very loud, very smartly-dressed American tourists on some sort of a literary conference were suddenly swelling the inside of the gatehouse, all starting to queue for keys to their borrowed college rooms. Posie saw another Porter, an older fellow this time, come out from the back of the Porter's Lodge. He was jangling a bunch of keys and looking harassed, obviously about to change places with Simpkins for the evening. Posie was suddenly desperate to be away; to be quiet and alone with her thoughts, to get ready for the formal dinner ahead of her.

She nodded. 'Thank you, Simpkins. Yes, please go ahead and ask Frank Bevans. I'm obliged to you. Thank you for the tips.'

Posie turned on her heel, but looked back just in time to see Simpkins disappearing under a crush of fashionable American pinstriped suits.

'Remember!' she heard him call out to her retreating back, 'Greenwood! It could be important!'

* * * *

Up in the smart blue guestroom in the Master's Lodge of Trinity College, Posie flung down her shopping bags and attempted to make a bit of order out of the chaos.

Her paper bags from Eaden Lilley's and Robert Sayle's were absolutely wet through and she extracted the Christmas presents inside carefully, inspecting them anxiously, hopeful that the inner packaging had proved a little more sturdy. Luckily the gauzy peach scarf she had bought for her best friend Dolly Price was still well protected by some sheets of expensive wrapping paper, and the solid silver rattles she had bought for each of Dolly and Rufus's twin daughters, the Honourable Bunny and Trixie Cardigeon, and also for her friend Inspector Lovelace's baby daughter, Phyllis, for whom she was Godmother, were thankfully impervious to the weather.

But everything else – an expensive tin of Lobster Bisque for her secretary Prudence, a book about allotment gardening for her business partner, Len, and a pure silk handkerchief for the Inspector – had suffered rain damage and looked very much the worse for wear.

Huffing and puffing Posie placed the ruined items on a chair nearest the fireplace and hoped for the best. She changed quickly out of her wet things and squeezed herself into a navy velour dress which was fortunately cut in the new style and made light of her curves. She wasn't in the mood to fawn over preparing her appearance for dinner: she made the best of her short hair and added a bit of lipstick, then sat down at her dressing table, her thoughts turning back to her brother Richard yet again.

Out came that strange short little letter. It was more than a year old now, from December 1921. It had been typed, and was postmarked 'Cambridge'.

Posie read it again, frowning as she did so.

Miss Parker,

I hope you don't mind my contacting you. I saw your name and details in The Times and I supposed you were Richard Parker's little sister. He always said you were a resourceful, clever girl. He was very proud of you back when I knew him.

The fact is, Richard left something behind in Cambridge. If you are interested in meeting me and finding out more, please send a reply to the Secretary of the Department of Botany, Downing Street. Mark it for the confidential attention of Harry Eden and they will see I get it.

With best wishes.

H.E.

And Posie had written back straightaway, as instructed, expressing her interest in the writer's news.

But then days and weeks and then months had passed

and nothing had come back. She had even gone so far as to investigate the identity of 'Harry Eden', only to have it confirmed by the university that no one registered under that name existed. She had drawn a blank.

She had even telegrammed the Secretary of the Botany Faculty, but she had received no reply either. Some days she dismissed the original letter as a joke, a fraud, a wind-up; other days she had worried about it constantly, about what the writer might possibly know about her brother which she didn't.

She planned to visit the Botany Department first thing tomorrow. If the search was entirely fruitless she would leave it and sure as bread was bread she could say she had at least *tried*.

She crammed the letter back into her bag and wrapped herself carefully in her warm red hat and coat and made her way to the Great Hall. Visitors to the college were expected to dine there at the candle-lit, long, shiny wooden tables which filled the hall. The Master's guests, like Posie, were accorded the double privilege of sitting at the 'High Table' along with the academic staff.

There weren't many women about. Trinity College was, like all the other old colleges in the university, just for men. Women couldn't take their degrees here, and if they wanted to study anything at all they had to take themselves off to an out-of-the-way college on the only hill in the whole city. They were depreciatively known in the newspapers as 'bluestockings', and viewed with equal amounts of awe and ridicule by differing members of the university, depending on who you spoke to.

Posie would never normally have been allowed to stay in the regular student accommodation in the college; that was reserved for male students and male visitors, but she *had* kindly been invited to stay in the altogether more comfortable surroundings of the centrally-located Master's Lodge by the kindly Master, who had known Richard, and had wanted to make Posie feel comfortable and welcome for her stay.

She felt a momentary tug at her heartstrings as she passed by her brother's old set of rooms on her way to eat in the Great Hall, and stifled the urge to cry. She focused instead on being business-like and methodical, and reminded herself to keep her eyes and ears open for clues as to Richard's last years at the college. Posie remembered Simpkins' recommendation to talk to Dr Greenwood. It was strange: Posie wracked her brains but she couldn't remember Richard ever having mentioned anyone called Greenwood. Other friends' names hovered tantalisingly, suspended in her memory forever, but she knew that most of Richard's Cambridge friends and colleagues were, like him, dead and buried, casualties of war.

Perhaps Dr Greenwood was a rare survivor. A last chance.

* * * *

But dinner was a disappointment.

Posie had no idea why Simpkins had directed her attention towards Dr Greenwood, or why he had warned her off Professor Somerjay, who turned out to be a first-class storyteller, funny and inspiring by turns, and who held the whole High Table captivated, riveted with suspense.

By contrast, Dr Greenwood, although very good-looking (if you liked your men bland and anodyne) was dull and peevish, and hugely pleased with himself, talking mainly about his publications and his recent boring appointment as Deputy Head of the Department of Botany. Posie was hugely surprised that someone like her brother, funny and devil-may-care about most things, could have been friends with such a stick-in-the-mud. Posie was bored all the way through the starter and the first course, and her attempts to talk about her brother with Dr Greenwood were politely rebuffed and avoided, so much so that she doubted he had ever really known Richard at all. Had Simpkins got his facts wrong somewhere along the lines?

Eating up her crème brûlée with gusto Posie decided to blow caution to the wind. The candles were flickering, the port wine was flowing and the clock was ticking. Posie decided that it was now or never. She took the year-old letter from Harry Eden out of her carpet bag.

'I say, Dr Greenwood. Would you mind taking a look at this for me?' She passed the paper across to the man quickly, before her nerve failed her.

'Do you happen to know a Harry Eden? I think you may be the only professional colleague and friend of my brother's left in the college here. Do you have any idea what the letter may be alluding to? What it was that Richard "left behind"? I'm just drawing endless blanks. Is there some connection to the Botany Department? The letter makes reference to a Secretary there…'

Dr Greenwood read the short letter in the light of one of the candles and Posie swore that she saw all the colour drain out of his handsome dark face in the dim light.

'I'm sorry,' Dr Greenwood smiled tightly, 'I haven't a clue what this letter is on about. Perhaps it was referring to some papers, or to a book which your brother was working on? Which might be worth something financially to you? Is that what you're after?'

He was talking very fast now, his hand clamped down over Posie's letter. 'I'm sorry to disappoint you if that's the case, but members of the Botany Department went through all of Richard's work after he died, and nothing valuable was found of that sort at all. Nothing which will get you money. So no, I have no idea what the letter is on about. Sorry.'

'And Harry Eden? Do you know him?'

Dr Greenwood pursed his lips in a thin line and shook his head quickly.

'I see. Well, thank you for clearing that up for me.'

He knows exactly what this letter is referring to, Posie thought to herself sharply. *Sure as bread is bread he knows, but he doesn't want me to find out. Why?* Could it be some brilliant new piece of research which Richard had been working on, and which Dr Greenwood was now passing off as his own?

And who the blazes was Harry Eden? Was he a former colleague? And where was he now, if that was the case? Had Harry Eden moved on, or died, or been silenced somehow? Or had he been disgraced? Dr Greenwood seemed a pretty unscrupulous sort, and if so, having Posie meddling about here into this matter would be most inconvenient.

Posie hadn't had time to be offended at Dr Greenwood's implication that she was simply after money, but her mind was racing sixteen to the dozen, trying to puzzle-piece out what Dr Greenwood could be hiding. She hadn't even considered the possibility that her brother might be on the verge of a new, secret discovery when he went off to war. It seemed that Dr Greenwood was protesting a little too much for her liking. Posie carefully extracted the letter from his hand with one sharp tug.

'Thank you for looking at it anyway,' she said politely.

They were interrupted by Professor Somerjay, leaning over, offering port.

'Posie Parker, isn't it? The famous woman Private Detective I've been reading all about in all the newspapers over the last year? Scotland Yard's right-hand gal, aren't you, kid? By Gad, if Richard could see his baby sister now! Quite the professional, aren't you?'

Posie laughed merrily and had the instant satisfaction of seeing Dr Greenwood's face turn even paler beside her.

'A detective?' Dr Greenwood asked, a laughing note

covering what sounded like a murmur of panic. 'You didn't tell me *that*.'

* * * *

Five

The next morning Posie woke early and dressed immediately.

For some reason she felt apprehensive and fidgety. To calm herself she watched the sunrise from her mullioned guestroom window in the Master's Lodge. The day promised to be cold, with yet more rain; the sky was a pink blur and the sun burned angrily at its very centre. Her room enjoyed a splendid view across the back of the college, across the sweep of the immaculate frost-covered lawns of the Master's Gardens, all the way down to the mist-covered River Cam. It was a scene straight from a Christmas card, but, in truth, Christmas cards and Christmas itself were very far from Posie's mind right now.

She decided on the spur of the moment to forgo breakfast downstairs with the Master and his wife and to take an early-morning walk instead in the direction of the Botany Department: she was crazily early, she knew, but she could always hang around waiting for a member of staff to arrive, or perhaps kill some time by walking along the Cam. Posie had already packed her overnight bag, re-packing her Christmas purchases as best she could. In fact, she was ready to leave Cambridge as soon as her visit to the Botany Department was over. The visit to Cambridge had certainly proved eventful enough already. Besides, she was itching to be back in her beloved London.

Leaving a scrawled note of thanks for the Master and taking her bags with her, Posie left the Lodge as quietly as she could, exiting out of a side door. The college clock was just striking seven o'clock.

Wrapped up warmly, she walked briskly down the neat frosty paths of Nevile's Court and away from the golden buildings of Trinity College. As she scurried along in the early-morning silence Posie thought she caught sight of a woman walking up ahead of her on the gravel path, just visible through the mist; a dark-haired woman in a vivid red coat, who turned once or twice at the sound of Posie's hob-nailed walking boots.

Who was walking around at this early hour in the Christmas holidays? And a woman too, in a place where they were certainly few and far between.

The sun was growing stronger now and the mist was lifting a little, and Posie heard the Chapel bells begin to ring. Perhaps the woman would stop and talk? Posie hurried on ahead, on over the neat little brick bridge over the Cam and on through the further set of lawns. She lost sight of the figure in red walking ahead of her.

Someone appeared in front of Posie, emerging suddenly through the ribbons of thin white mist rising off the river. It was the bowler-hatted Porter from yesterday, Simpkins. He was wearing the same uniform as on the day before, a thin black waistcoat over rolled-up white shirtsleeves. His lack of a coat or scarf made Posie, who always felt the cold despite her permanent insulation, shiver profusely.

'Miss Parker? Good morning! Looks like we'll be having more rain today, more's the pity. Doesn't look like it'll be a white Christmas, does it? Shame!'

Simpkins did a half-bow and passed Posie a brown envelope.

'Your photograph, Miss,' said Simpkins brightly. 'The

one of the fella you were asking about? It's in the envelope.'

'Ah, yes.' Posie had almost forgotten about Felicity Fyne and the case of Dr Winter; she was so immersed in her own thoughts about Richard. 'Thank you. Any joy?'

'Well, yes, actually.' Simpkins looked pleased with himself and drew himself up to his full height, which wasn't much.

'I tracked Frank Bevans down to his regular, the Dog and Ball on the Cherry Hinton Road. He said he definitely saw your man yesterday lunchtime. Tall blonde fella, wearing a gown. He left Trinity College about half-past one. Frank said that the fella seemed in rather a hurry; kept his head down, as if he didn't fancy being recognised.'

'Oh?' Posie's heart was pounding. This news meant that Dr Winter *was* alive after all. Could it be?

She was astounded: she had expected a negative outcome, not a positive identification. Her senses were immediately drill-sharp and she found herself wishing that she had been able to question Bevans herself. After all, the college got a lot of visitors, and yesterday had been no exception to that rule. Just how accurate was this man Bevans' memory, and how could you trust the word of a man you had never met, anyway? It was second-hand hearsay evidence.

Simpkins broke in on her train of thought:

'Two points, Miss. Frank Bevans said to mention them to you particularly.'

'Oh? I was just thinking that maybe I should talk to Bevans myself. No offence intended.'

'None taken. But that won't be possible, Miss. Frank Bevans is indisposed for the time being. He can't get around as much as he'd like to at the moment, as much as he did in the past. You'll have to make do with me. He told me to mention that your fella had a very bad limp; the right leg dragging. And the second point was that the man was wearing a black academic gown, but Frank said there was summit strange about it. It wasn't a university gown, that's for sure.'

'Really?'

Posie's mind was racing: the detail of the limp was new; she didn't recall *that* from her dealings with Dr Winter or from her conversation with Felicity the day before. But the other detail given by Bevans was very similar to that which Felicity Fyne had reported – she had said Dr Winter had worn a black gown and that he had looked dusty, or *shabby*, in fact, when she had spied him.

'I'm much obliged to you, Simpkins.'

He nodded and made to move off in the direction of the college, when something else occurred to Posie.

'I say, did you pass a woman in a bright red coat on your way in just now?'

'Mrs Greenwood, you mean, Miss? Yes, of course. She's our resident college beauty, if you don't mind my saying so. She walks this way most mornings; it's the quickest route to get to her job. She lives in the college with her husband. You remember? Her husband is Dr Greenwood, who you met last night at dinner. She works on Downing Street. Goes in early.'

Posie couldn't believe that Dr Greenwood hadn't mentioned his wife once during the long, boring dinner.

'He didn't talk about her then, to you?'

Posie shook her head, shifting her bags.

'I'm not surprised,' said the Porter, his head on one side in a knowing fashion.

'It's all a bit tricky. Well, if that's everything, Miss, have a good day.'

* * * *

When she reached the Department of Botany on Downing Street, Posie saw that the shutters were still closed and the night-lights were still burning in the porch.

Posie walked around the grand red-brick building with its many long white-stone windows, wondering whether to wait out of politeness for a member of staff to arrive, or whether to give up now and catch the train home. It was all needle-in-a-haystack territory anyway: she didn't even have a definite contact person who could help her here, just that strange name – Harry Eden – and *that* might all come to nothing, if he had died or left the place.

Just then, on her second lap around the building, Posie happened to look through the ground-floor window nearest the main door of the porch. The windows of this room were unshuttered, and inside, a blur of bright red could be glimpsed. It resolved itself into the shape of a woman removing her coat, then sitting down at a wooden desk and angling a desk-light over a thick blue tome of papers before her.

Mrs Greenwood.

How opportune! Was she an academic too? And if so, Posie felt a mixture of joy and admiration that a woman was managing to pursue an academic career in this totally male-dominated place.

In a jiffy Posie had rapped on the window. She waved frantically when Mrs Greenwood looked up, caught unawares; half-surprised, half-anxious.

'Can you help me?' Posie mouthed through the glass.

* * * *

Inside, the large office was dark and messy. The room was a reception of some sort, with a small velvet couch and a coffee-table, all strewn with papers. There was paperwork all over the place, stacked up in great toppling piles rising up on every surface. Charts and graphs and photographs covered the cork pin-boards which ran around the walls. The beginnings of a fire in the grate were just starting to warm the high-ceilinged room, which was freezing cold.

'So, what can I do for you?'

Mrs Greenwood was unfriendly. But Posie was convinced that her curt manner belied some sort of anxiety. But anxiety about what?

Posie explained quickly who she was and why she had come, and passed across her business card and the letter from Harry Eden, while all the time studying the open blue leather-tooled tome gripped tight under Mrs Greenwood's hands on the desk in front of her. It appeared to be a great mass of research and graphs and hand-painted illustrations with small labels attached to them. The tiny graphs looked horribly familiar somehow, and the sight of them there brought back clear memories, like echoes rippling through time. Richard had drawn up diagrams such as these, and the sight of what could very well have been one of his sketches peeping out of a page gave Posie quite a shock.

'No, I can't help you,' said Mrs Greenwood certainly and quickly, looking over at the doorway behind Posie as she spoke. 'I've never seen this letter before and I've never heard of the man it alludes to. It must be a hoax. I'm sorry for you. You've had a wasted journey.'

But as she passed back the letter, Posie noticed how the woman's hands shook. *Just what on earth is going on here*, she thought to herself.

She noticed smaller details too: the sallow duskiness of Mrs Greenwood's skin and the silky dense blackness of her hair, hinting at an oriental descent which must be her inheritance somewhere down the line; the intense exotic beauty of her great purple eyes set within a face which spoke of other continents and other languages. But most of all Posie noticed the ugly bruise which had spread, bloom-like in all its yellow and green splendour across that lovely dark face, from forehead to chin.

Fine, Posie thought to herself, *I'll have to play it like this if that's how she wants it. But sure as bread is bread I'll get to the bottom of this.*

She vowed that if the Greenwoods were using Richard's notes or research without permission she would create merry hell for them. Perhaps he really had been on the verge of some wonderful new breakthrough: found some new ingredient for a miracle drug? Mrs Greenwood was up to something illicit, Posie was sure of it. Probably hand in glove with her insufferably boring husband, too, no doubt.

But who on earth had Harry Eden been?

Just then what seemed like a crowd of men swung in through the door to the office, all taking off their thick winter coats and hanging them on a coat-rack in the corner, and changing into their academic gowns for work. Posie saw that Dr Greenwood was among the people in the group, but that he made no attempt to welcome Posie or to introduce her to his staff, as Richard's sister. In fact, he shot Posie a look of barely-concealed irritation and dislike. She was left standing foolishly in the middle of the room, feeling awkward and out of place. She couldn't have imagined Richard ever having worked in this place; it seemed so bereft of any joy. Dr Greenwood stormed over to his wife.

'Any post for me today, Evangeline?'

His wife shook her head and carefully placed her large blue leather book in a drawer in her desk, but not before Posie had seen the fear in her eyes.

Mrs Greenwood went across to what Posie now saw was a series of wire pigeonholes on the left-hand side of the office where she retrieved a few pieces of post, deliv-ering them directly and meekly into the hands of the men they were intended for. Posie was confused, until she saw that one of the pigeonholes was inscribed with:

E. Greenwood
Acting Secretary of the Department of Botany

So Mrs Greenwood was not an academic after all. She was the secretary.

And suddenly it dawned on Posie that Mrs Greenwood must have been the very secretary with whom Posie had communicated last year about the strange letter from Harry Eden.

So she was definitely lying. But why? But Posie realised it would have to wait for another time, another place. She had reached an impasse. She would have to try and get Mrs Greenwood alone somehow.

Dr Greenwood had crossed the large room and Posie saw that he had taken up residence at a large, leather-covered desk in the opposite corner of the room to his wife, but in a position where he could watch her every single move, and where he was able to watch the movements of everyone else who came in and out of the room. He seated himself at his desk in an important fashion and stared at Posie, seemingly willing her to leave. It occurred to Posie that Dr Greenwood must have obtained this job for his wife so he could keep an eye on her all day long. Like a rare bird trapped in a strange cage.

There was nothing for it but to go.

As she turned to leave, Posie noticed how Mrs Greenwood wouldn't meet her eye. Instead, she sat mutely ticking off some boring administrative lists, the fat blue tome of research now banished out of sight.

So Mrs Greenwood was scared of her own husband; that

68

must be it. That would account for the bruise. And the cowed look, too.

Posie shivered despite the warmth of her coat. She raised her hand insincerely in farewell, the uselessness of her trip to the Botany Department just sinking in.

'Goodbye then, Dr Greenwood, and Mrs Greenwood too. It's been a real pleasure.'

And the irony of the words tasted very bitter in her mouth indeed.

* * * *

PART TWO
Wednesday 20th and Thursday 21st December, 1922

Six

The Florence Restaurant on Rupert Street in Soho, London, was heaving with noisy pre-Christmas revellers. Marzipan-scented wafts of some fancy Italian liqueur which Posie didn't recognise hung over the place, and people seemed in the mood to celebrate.

Posie had booked a table for lunch and for once, amazingly, she was early. The date had been in the diary for a good few weeks. She waited for her lunch-date to arrive, eating some crispy Italian candied peanuts which had been left temptingly next to her plate, and studying the three identical Christmas cards which she had lined up on the snow-white tablecloth in front of her.

As requested, Felicity Fyne had sent the two earlier cards from the blackmailer, and Posie had already spent an inordinate amount of time looking at them all on the previous afternoon, on her return from Cambridge.

She had been willing clues to fly up off them, but she was none the wiser now, save for feeling like she knew the blackmailer's words off by heart. The only differences she could ascertain between the cards were the dates on them, and the fact that the first two cards were specific in mentioning the amount – thirty pounds – required to satisfy the blackmailer's demands. But something about the cards bothered her, pulled at something in her mind that she couldn't quite place.

Posie sighed: this case involving Dr Winter had taken up all of her day yesterday, and was threatening to take over the whole run-up to Christmas, too.

She had spent part of yesterday at the office of the Imperial War Graves Commission, checking through their records for the details of the death and the burial place of Dr Winter. She had found general details about the bombing of the Clearing Station on Valentine's Day, 1918, as Felicity Fyne had mentioned, but Dr Winter was simply recorded as 'missing, presumed dead', and there was no grave listed for him.

This was in total contrast to the other members of the medical unit who had died in the blast, including Dulcie Deane, whose death was confirmed and whose place of burial was listed as being next to the Clearing Station in a small cemetery there, together with a complicated set of grid references for locating her grave.

Posie had then spoken to the Red Cross Organisation and had asked for any details they might have about the bombing of the Clearing Station, but all she was told was that there had been 'no survivors'.

Posie had also had the bright idea of badgering the Royal College of Surgeons in Lincoln's Inn Fields to confirm whether or not a Dr William Winter was listed as actively practicing on their records at present, but they had politely refused her request, adding that unless it was a proper 'police enquiry' they could not release any such information. Posie had asked for details of Dr Winter's father too, to see if he was still practicing medicine up in Glasgow, but they wouldn't release any information on him either. Beyond this, Posie could not go.

It seemed that everywhere she was turning she faced dead ends.

Posie had come full circle and was now convinced that

Felicity Fyne *had* seen her own husband in the flesh; that the evidence of the Porter, Bevans, was accurate, and that Dr Winter was, far from being dead, alive and well. She felt sure she was dealing with one of these complicated double-identity cases; that Dr Winter had somehow survived that terrible bombing and had vanished into thin air. But how? And why? It also seemed to Posie more than ever that this case demanded a two-pronged attack: that as well as finding Dr Winter, she needed to find the blackmailer and to stop them in their tracks.

Thwarted by the Royal College of Surgeons, she had sent off a telegram direct to the Glasgow Royal Infirmary, hopeful that the elder Dr Winter still worked there, asking him for an interview.

It seemed incomprehensible to Posie that a man who was an only child could cut off all contact with his parents, even if he was potentially in hiding from his past and his previous life. Perhaps the elder Dr Winter had heard from his son and would be able to help; to offer Posie some information.

Posie looked up and saw the large-headed, tall, swinging figure of Chief Inspector Richard Lovelace of New Scotland Yard silhouetted at the doorway of the restaurant, removing his black homburg hat and hand-knitted brown scarf in one quick, practised movement.

'Posie!' he called out cheerfully, bowling over and taking the chair opposite her own. 'It's been a little while. Thanks for the lunch invite, and Merry Christmas, almost!'

He passed across a box of Fortnum's Rose Creams, wrapped in pink foil. 'I know these are your favourites. And I probably won't see you before Christmas itself.'

Posie laughed and thanked him and gave the Chief Inspector a small parcel containing the silver rattle for his baby daughter. She didn't have anything for him personally: the lunch at the Florence was her present instead.

Ordering quickly, Posie surveyed the Inspector. He had

that tired creased look about the eyes which only sleepless nights with a small baby can bring, but he looked well on it, too. His stance was of one at the pinnacle of both his personal and professional life, which was, as it happened, fairly accurate: he had been promoted to Chief Inspector only eight months previously, and had become a first-time father at almost exactly the same time. Posie smiled, happy for him.

She had worked with the maverick Inspector on several cases before, and they had helped each other out on numerous occasions, trading information and sharing methods in a wholly unorthodox manner which somehow, against the odds, seemed to work. On one memorable occasion Posie had even pretended to be the Inspector's wife on a highly dangerous undercover operation, which had proved risky for all concerned. It would be fair to say that the Inspector was Posie's only really trusted contact at New Scotland Yard, although his Sergeants, Binny and Rainbird, had proven useful not infrequently.

Over a Tuscan wild-boar stew which seemed peculiarly out-of-place on the winter streets of Soho, Inspector Lovelace enthused about the charms of little Phyllis Lovelace, who, Posie was amused to observe, was obviously the centre of her doting father's universe.

'Golly, hark at me,' Inspector Lovelace stopped, embarrassed, swigging from a celebratory glass of Tuscan red, 'all I'm talking about is the baby! I forget, you're not really a "baby person", are you?' But before Posie could remark that she had never had the chance to be or to become a 'baby person', he had sailed on enthusiastically:

'So what's new at the Grape Street Bureau? Len behaving himself, is he? Any spicy cases on?'

Posie shook her head, outlining a few of the bigger cases she was working on, but without much enthusiasm. In truth, the case of Dr Winter was perplexing her and consuming all her thoughts.

She wrestled with whether or not to speak to him about her visit to Cambridge, especially as Felicity Fyne had said she didn't want any police involvement, but the combination of the tart red wine, the delicious food and the party atmosphere of the Florence Restaurant loosened her tongue. Besides, Inspector Lovelace was discreet to his very core, and Posie felt that she needed someone to bounce ideas off. In fact, she felt utterly stuck. Where on earth would she find Dr Winter if he didn't want to be found? Besides, if she couldn't speak about it to the Inspector, who could she speak to?

She found herself quickly outlining the little case over a large portion of the excellent tiramisu which the restaurant was justly famous for, and, surprisingly, she found herself eagerly looking to Inspector Lovelace for what to do next. He rubbed his large hand over his gingery, stubbly chin thoughtfully.

'Tricky,' he said eventually, pursing his lips. 'If a fella wants to go to ground, there's not much you can do about it. I see it time and time again. Easy enough after the chaos of the Great War. It's more than likely he doesn't want to be found. *If* you're convinced it really *was* him, that is.'

'But a person can't simply just disappear into thin air!' Posie insisted heatedly. 'How do you live? How do you eat? You need money. There are barely enough jobs in the country right now as it is, with unemployment at an all-time high, even if you *do* have the right paperwork! And Dr Winter doesn't even have that! His wife kept all of his documents so that she could claim her War Widow's Pension. Officially he's dead.'

Inspector Lovelace gave Posie a meaningful glance. 'We both know that documents can be faked, Posie. We've both dealt with clever forgery gangs before.'

'But this is a highly trained surgeon! How can he work without the right paperwork?'

'A pseudonym perhaps? We've both dealt with those before, too…'

A thought struck her.

'I say, you couldn't do me a favour, could you...?'

The Inspector groaned, but good-humouredly. After all, it was almost Christmas, and he found himself agreeing to call the Royal College of Surgeons to ask them to confirm whether Dr William Winter was currently on their books as an acting surgeon.

'I'll telephone you this afternoon,' he promised. 'But I can see this case is eating you up, and that's always dangerous. I know there's a personal connection, but don't let it get to you too much. So much of what happened in the war was so sad; it's sometimes best for people to have a fresh start. Don't deny this poor fella that. Perhaps he had some sort of a breakdown? Shell-shock after the sights he saw, maybe? Happened to the best of us, you know. *I* still dream about all the noise.'

'I don't care about fresh starts,' Posie said hotly, fishing in her carpet bag for her purse to pay the bill as a smart waiter hovered discreetly nearby. 'I just want to find out *the truth.*'

When she looked up again she saw the Inspector was looking intently at the three Christmas cards Felicity Fyne had received from the blackmailer, together with their envelopes. A familiar look was playing about his eyes: he had caught the scent of the mystery and was hooked.

'You know what?' the Inspector said, interest now rising in his voice, 'these letters were all sent from this very street. Here in Soho. The Rupert Street Post Office. How bizarre is that? What a coincidence! In the whole of London we happen to eat lunch in the very place where these were posted from! Shall we take a gander and amble past the Post Office itself?'

Posie privately thought that the coincidence was nothing special. But she agreed: after all, she didn't have anything else particularly pressing to get back for, and with no other leads as yet, she felt like letting her mind wander.

Outside on the pavement the thick, grey afternoon air was growing chill and a London fog was rising, wrapping itself around pedestrians like a soft, damp blanket. The bitter cold hit them. It was growing dark already although it was only half-past two.

Posie shivered and took the Inspector's arm when he offered it. They walked along the street in a companionable silence. Rupert Street was dimly lit with street-lamps and was full of small cafés and inauspicious restaurants catering for office workers. Some of the buildings were obviously brand new and were roughly built, as if they had been put up in a real hurry, and some of the spaces facing the road were totally empty, protected by big corrugated-iron hoardings, as if the buildings which had previously been there had been ripped down in a frantic race against the clock and were waiting to be re-assembled.

'There was a Zeppelin raid here in the war,' said the Inspector by way of quick explanation as they crossed over a piece of curling, soggy wet duckboard on the pavement outside the Post Office. 'A good many shops and buildings were hit. Must have been awful.'

The Post Office was small and dim and nothing particularly special. A line of nondescript muffled-up office workers were queuing to reach a wooden counter with partitions, and a gaggle of white-hooded nurses were taking up the rear. Most were carrying last-minute Christmas parcels done up with string.

'Dead end,' said Posie rather huffily. 'What exactly are we hoping to achieve? We can't very well ask in *here* if anyone remembers who sent this card last week, or in the two previous years. They must get hundreds of Christmas cards posted from here every day! It's not as if there's anything special about the card or the writing, either!'

They left the Post Office together.

'Brrr! It's icy out here!' The Inspector shivered, nestling his chin into his thick brown scarf. 'You're right: it's a dead end. If I think of anything else I'll let you know, but I have to say I'm not hopeful for you.'

Posie said goodbye, turning office-wards, not liking to admit that privately she totally agreed with the Inspector's pessimistic view.

* * * *

Seven

The fire in her small office at the Grape Street Bureau blazed lustily throughout the afternoon and Posie sat lost in thought at her desk with Mr Minks, her beloved Siamese cat, resting warily upon her knee. Outside her window the sky was now pitch black.

When Prudence Smythe, Posie's highly efficient secretary, popped her head around the door and announced Inspector Lovelace's telephone call, Posie nearly jumped out of her skin.

'As we thought,' the Inspector's voice crackled down the line.

'Not a dicky-bird at the Royal College of Surgeons. No mention of a Dr William Winter since before the war. Nothing. I checked out any possible pseudonyms by using the date of birth and area of medical expertise you gave me, but there was nothing doing. Frosty lot, aren't they, doctors? I felt like a naughty schoolboy asking them for the information. I half expected to be given lines to be written on the chalkboard as a punishment! Being a Chief Inspector seemed to cut no mustard, either. So he's definitely dead, your doctor, or else he's doing something else…'

'A *chalkboard*? Did you just say?'

But Posie wasn't really listening to the Inspector's answer. Her mind was working ten to the dozen, racing helter-skelter over a possible theory. *He's doing something else...*

She remembered what Felicity had said; that the doctor had been wearing a long black university gown, and that he had looked odd; that he *looked sort of dusty*.

But, based on the observations of the keen-eyed and mysterious Porter, Bevans, it seemed that the gown Dr Winter had been wearing had been different to other university gowns. So what if the gown Dr Winter had been wearing was in fact a *Schoolmaster's* gown, such as those worn by hundreds of men who taught boys in private schools up and down the country?

To the untrained eye, or to someone far away, it would look like a university gown, but to someone who saw university gowns hundreds of times a day – someone such as a Porter – it would be instantly recognisable as being different. But it would have made a perfect disguise for Dr Winter at the Memorial Service, allowing him to blend in. It was virtually an invisibility cloak. And didn't it make sense that the dust on the black gown was in fact *chalk* dust, which was known to be fiendishly difficult to remove?

'That's it!' Posie breathed certainly.

'Eh?'

'He *is* doing something else. Change of plan!'

The Inspector groaned. 'I knew I should have left this well alone.'

'One last favour. Only one. I promise.'

'Go on.'

'Something you just said made me think that perhaps Dr Winter is living incognito, even at the cost of having given up his profession. I think, Chief Inspector, that he's working as a Schoolmaster. We need to find him!'

'How on earth...? No, never mind. What is it you want me to do for you, Posie?'

'Do you have access to some sort of central compendium of all the Schoolmasters and Schoolmistresses currently working in the country?'

'No! Of course I don't. Not at my fingertips, anyway. Who would? I don't think there *is* such a central directory. If this fella wants to stay hidden he won't have made the daft mistake of joining the Trade Union for teachers, or the Association for Schoolmasters, or the Teachers' Registration Council. Teachers don't have to join those associations, unfortunately. That would make things too easy for us. So it's needle-in-a-haystack territory, Posie. Yet again.'

Posie's mind was scrambling but the Inspector got in quicker:

'Unless…'

'Yes?'

The Inspector sighed:

'Unless I get a couple of my lads to scoot over to the Board of Education on Whitehall; go through the records for all the schools in the country. You see, schools have to declare when new teachers come and start working for them; their pay-scale, their date of birth and so on. The records should be up to date, particularly since this bally Geddes Act means that teachers' pay is getting slashed, and it all needs to be recorded *somewhere*. But this Dr Winter has probably got a pseudonym. It could take forever.'

'No, I don't think it will take forever,' Posie said certainly, thinking of the Dr Winter she had worked with. She did not think he was imaginatively inclined, definitely not the sort of person who could come up with an exotic new name for himself.

'Just check the new teachers for the year 1918, when Dr Winter supposedly died. That's when he would have started to work, I'm sure of it. Just get your men to check *private* schools for boys, they're the only places where those black gowns are compulsory for Masters; that will narrow down the search a lot. And get your lads to check under the name "Winter", of course, but also polar opposites too: "summer", "autumn", "spring". Golly, and derivations of winter, too: "Snow", "White", "Frost" He won't have wandered far from his real name, I'm sure of it.'

'I have his date of birth already, but is there any particular subject he'd be teaching?'

'Mnn, not sure. The sciences? That's the nearest thing I can think of next to medicine, isn't it?'

'You don't ask much, do you? Good job it's Christmas and I'm feeling charitable. I'll have to say it's official police business, which we both know is a lie. My lads could be over there at the Board of Education for a long time. I'll get a couple of my best Constables on the job and tell them to take a thermos flask of tea over with them. They'll come back to you when we know more, hopefully tomorrow morning. I hope this isn't a mare's nest, Posie. Tell me there's method in the madness – you're not just going on some fantastical "hunch" – please?'

Posie ignored the question and stroked the cat instead.

'Thank you, Inspector. Thank you a hundred times. I owe you, big time.'

'*Again*,' said Inspector Lovelace smartly as he rang off.

****

Just as Posie was heading back into her own office, a Post Office messenger-boy knocked and came through the glass-stencilled main office door.

'Telegram!' he announced cheerily, proffering his cap, hopeful for a Christmas tip. Prudence Smythe, so supremely frugal that Len Irving swore she used their tea ration five times over, shook a small desk-sized Christmas tree in his direction angrily.

'Get away with you! No tips here! You get paid a work-ing wage by the Post Office, you cheeky scoundrel!'

Posie passed a coin over to the lad and took the telegram, to the loud tut-tutting of her secretary. It was from Professor Winter, up in Glasgow.

She read:

YOUR TELEGRAM JUST CAUGHT ME.

LUCKILY FOR YOU I'M ABOUT TO BOARD THE OVERNIGHT SLEEPER TO LONDON FOR A MEDICAL CONFERENCE. IF YOU WANT TO DISCUSS MY SON, MEET ME AT 7.30 SHARP TOMORROW MORNING AT KING'S CROSS STA-TION, PLATFORM 5.

YOU CAN WALK WITH ME AND WE'LL TALK AS WE GO. DON'T BE LATE - I WON'T WAIT FOR YOU.

PROFESSOR G. WINTER

Posie sighed in relief. At last – a break – a few odds and ends were coming together. All her hard work might just be paying off, after all.

Never mind that the Professor sounded unfriendly and frosty in his telegram – Felicity Fyne had described him as a cold fish, and that was certainly saying something – wasn't it hopeful that he had bothered to write back at all?

Posie found she was considering all of this and playing absent-mindedly with the small desk-sized Christmas tree when Len Irving, her business partner, came crashing noisily into the office. He was laden down with Christmas presents wrapped in brightly coloured papers. He was also managing to shake out a huge umbrella at the same time, causing icy water droplets to spill out across the carpet.

'Wotcha, Po! Terrible weather out there. Freezing fog and now rain! Chills the bones! And talking of cold old bones, how's your dead doctor doing?'

Posie rolled her eyes heavenwards: Len could be *very* annoying at times, almost akin to a small child. But there was no getting away from the fact that, what with his dark good looks and his near-permanent smile, he was devilishly handsome, and charming to boot, which had got him forgiven hundreds of times over.

Len had been Posie's almost-boyfriend for a while there back in 1921, before he had got sudden cold feet and married his childhood sweetheart, Aggie, instead, in a sudden whirlwind wedding abroad. At the time, Posie had found Len's actions utterly incomprehensible and cruel; salt had most definitely been rubbed into the open wound of her broken heart and Posie had wondered if they could continue to work professionally together. But they had struggled on through.

Since then Len had become a father to a baby son, Alfred, the apple of his eye, and Posie, well, Posie had Alaric now: as much as anyone could 'have' Alaric, that was.

'Actually, I don't think the doctor is dead, after all. I think he's in hiding, for whatever reason.'

'Oh?' said Len, raiding one of the bags he was carrying and producing some Eccles cakes in a green-and-white striped Lyons Cornerhouse wrapper.

'You'll find him then, poor fella. He can't stay hidden for long with you on the case, can he? Want one?' He waved the cakes first at Prudence, who accepted with a slight blush, for Len still had that effect on her after almost two years, and then at Posie, who shook her head, but not altogether convincingly.

'Can't. Thanks, though. I had a delicious Italian lunch with old Lovelace. My Christmas present to the Inspector.'

'*Chief* Inspector,' cut in Prudence insufferably from

behind her typewriter, between mouthfuls of flaky pastry. Posie rolled her eyes; their secretary was a terrible stickler for titles.

'Coo-ee! That sounds nice.' Len was reclining on the sofa in front of the main fireplace of the waiting room, stuffing his face happily.

'I'm looking for a nice place to take Aggie to for the New Year. You know, a slap-up treat. We haven't really been out since the baby was born. We'll leave Alfred with Aggie's mother for the night and I'll take her up town. It can't be too expensive, mind. Where was the place again?'

Len had thrown his beloved camera and all his parcels over the floor and coffee-table. Good job they weren't expecting any clients just yet, Posie thought to herself huffily, although she was aware that it was the mention of Len's wife's name which had made her feel sour, if truth be told, and not the state of the waiting room.

'Oh, it was "the Florence", if you must know,' Posie replied with a touch of ill grace.

'Over on Rupert Street? It was quite famous before the war, wasn't it? Quite the celebrity hang-out in its day.'

'Yep, that's the one. I hadn't been there in a long while. I'd forgotten how badly damaged the street was by the bombing in the war. It's still not repaired. It makes the whole place feel quite run-down. I don't think it would meet the high standards of your Aggie, so I wouldn't bother if I was you.'

'Ah, well. We'll see about that,' mused Len, oblivious to the sarcasm underpinning her words. He stretched out lazily. A warm fug had settled over his face as if he were recalling something extra special from days long gone.

'*I* remember Rupert Street.'

'Oh yes?' Posie said without interest. The evening post had just arrived and Prudence was sorting through it hastily, checking her wristwatch, wanting to leave on time. She passed Posie a couple of letters and filed the others with her own inimitable speed in the different wire baskets on her desk. Prudence gathered up her string shopping bag stuffed to the gunnels and bade both Len and Posie a swift goodnight, a couple of library books tucked under her arm.

Posie turned to her post. The first letter was from an elderly woman whom Posie had been working for in Harrogate. It was a simple thank you. The second, in bright red ink, was unfamiliar. She started to rip the second letter open.

'Yes,' continued Len dreamily. 'It was a nurse. She was a stunner.'

'*Sorry?* What?' Posie pulled out an oblong card with an expensive gold border, covered in spidery red handwriting.

Len sighed. 'I was just telling you that I went out with a nurse just before the war. She lived in that big hostel for nurses on Rupert Street. I had a devil of a time seeing her though; what with her crazy shifts and then the strict curfews in place at that hostel. There was a bulldog of a woman warden there on the door, I remember. Many was the time I tried to sneak through and failed.'

Posie gave Len a withering glance. She tried to look like she didn't care, but the details of his former love-life did still interest her, unfortunately.

'Well thanks for sharing that, Len. How illuminating. And what happened to her, this nurse of yours?'

'Dunno.' Len shrugged. 'I wanted to look her up after the war, but I couldn't, could I? I was gutted at the time.'

Posie rolled her eyes: 'I'm sure you got over it easily enough and moved on. Does Aggie know about the nurse? I thought *she* was your "before, during and after" the war?'

Len reddened, perhaps realising his insensitivity. He murmured something about having some work to do, and lurched off into his office.

Posie took his place gratefully on the couch and Mr Minks jumped up and joined her in front of the fire, curling around her legs, wrecking her good ten denier stockings like usual. She turned with interest to the oblong card. It was short and to the point, and utterly surprising:

Miss Parker,

We met on Tuesday in Cambridge. Please forgive my rudeness then. I will explain all when I see you again. If you would be kind enough to pay me a visit, I think you will understand.

Could you come to Cambridge this Friday, 22nd December? I very much hope so as I have something to show you. Say, two o'clock outside King's College?

Please don't reply to this letter, even if you can't come.

If you DO visit I will be delighted; if you do not, all it will have cost me will be a short wait outside a beautiful building.

With best wishes,

Evangeline Greenwood.

Posie stared into the middle distance, lost in thought. There was fear here too, hidden behind the showy red ink.

But there was something else, something like defiance, and, even more strangely, a sort of pride. And what on earth was it that Mrs Greenwood wanted to 'show' Posie, which meant she would have to make all the effort to trog up to Cambridge yet again? Was it the potential breakthrough research which Richard might have been working on before the war, which Dr Greenwood had got his hands on and was acting so cagily about? How come Mrs Greenwood was in a position to show Posie it now, when she hadn't been on Tuesday? And why couldn't Posie see whatever it was *here*, from the comfort of London?

She sighed: she didn't really fancy going up there again, and she had plenty on here in London in the run-up to Christmas, but there was nothing for it. Besides, if she didn't go, she might never hear from Evangeline Greenwood again, and now more than ever, Posie was convinced that Evangeline Greenwood held the key to unlocking the mystery of Richard Parker's final years.

* * * *

Posie fed Mr Minks his usual bit of best quality chicken and locked up at the Grape Street Bureau. She hurried home. Outside her flat in Museum Chambers, next to the British Museum and just around the corner from the office, three or four revellers strolled along the pavement, slightly the worse for wear, off to a Christmas party in fancy dress. They emerged out of the freezing fog like jolly phantoms.

It wasn't late, only seven o'clock, and normally this stretch of Bloomsbury-meets-the-West-End was busy with theatre-goers and shoppers, but the majority of people had packed up work for Christmas already, and escaped to the country, or wherever it was people went to when they had a real family to go home to.

'Merry Christmas, lovey!' shouted out one of the party-goers. To Posie's surprise it was a burly man, dressed in a flimsy female nurse's uniform.

'You too.' Posie nodded politely. She fished around in her bag for her keys, thinking how much easier it would be if Mr Minks had decided to move with her around the corner when she had bought her large flat, rather than stubbornly insisting on staying on at the office. Still, he was an old cat now and he didn't ask for much, so she humoured him.

Alaric was in. Posie could see the light spilling out from under her front door when she got out of the birdcage lift.

She felt suddenly light and joyful, and found herself looking forward to the evening ahead, hastily squirting herself with a dash of parma violet and dabbing a bit of pink greasepaint on her lips. She put her key in the lock, and swung in, ready to tell him about the improbable sight of the man dressed as a nurse.

But she stopped as soon as she saw the hallway strewn with paper, and Alaric, head in hands, madly roving backwards and forwards in the room he used as both his bedroom and study when he was staying in London. It was a scene of first-rate chaos. Bikram, Alaric's liver-coloured Pointer dog, sat patiently in a basket in the corner, pretending to sleep. It looked the best approach.

Too late Posie remembered that Alaric had been asked to give a big lecture, the Christmas address, on Friday at the Royal Geographical Society in town, for which they were paying him a handsome fee. He always left things to the last minute, and this looked worse than usual.

She decided to leave Alaric to it. Posie was hungry, too, and it looked like she'd be eating alone; a scratch meal for one, just like back in the old days. She fetched some cheese and biscuits and sat on the floor of her calm, uncluttered, pale green-painted sitting room, closing the door softly behind her.

The flat was decidedly free of the many Christmassy decorations which were tacked up in gaudy abundance over at the Grape Street Bureau, mainly at Prudence's insistence, but Posie had put up one tiny green tree, bought for a small fortune at Holborn Tube Station from a grocer up for the day from Kent. It was tastefully decorated now with just a few silver baubles bought at Liberty on Regent Street, and underneath it sat one neatly-wrapped Christmas present for Alaric, from her. The present was a book about city-beekeeping, and Posie had spent weeks looking for something suitable. When she had chanced upon the book in Foyles on the Charing Cross Road she had snapped it up at once, even though it had been pricey. Alaric had spent much of his twenties and thirties keeping bees in the grounds of his ancestral home, Boynton Hall, and had become justly renowned for his honey.

Since a disaster the year before when most of his hives had perished, he had been building them up again both back at Boynton Hall in the country, and also installing twelve hives on the roof of Museum Chambers, facing out over the British Museum, for when he was in London. It was early days yet but his attempts at city-beekeeping had seemed rather experimental so far and he had complained to Posie that it was all rather unchartered territory. Posie hoped her little gift would provide some handy hints and advice.

So far the gift looked a little lonely under the tree and hadn't been joined by a 'matching' present from Alaric to Posie. In fact, she had no idea whether Alaric had even noticed the tree, let alone his present. Had he even noticed it was about to be Christmas?

She sighed huffily, and as she munched away on her cheddar she wished she had taken one of Len's Eccles cakes for a dessert, they had looked so very tempting.

Posie thought of Len now, too, which she didn't permit herself to do very often. Would *he* have bought her a Christmas present if they were still a couple? He was so infuriating sometimes… a *nurse*! A *stunner*! Had he ever described *her* as a stunner to anyone? It seemed unlikely, somehow.

And now she had nurses on the brain, Posie thought to herself crossly. How many times had she seen a nurse, or heard one mentioned today? Too many times!

And suddenly, and with a sharp and horrible sense of clarity, an unwelcome thought planted itself firmly in Posie's head. Could it be? Her thoughts tumbled over each other in a mad rush:

A nurse. In a hostel on Rupert Street.

A nurse who posted letters from the Rupert Street Post Office.

A nurse who knew secrets. Secrets which were supposed to be dead and buried. A blackmailer.

Almost as if she were sleepwalking, Posie found herself padding along the parquet-floored corridor and entering her own bedroom and opening the big dark wooden cupboard where she kept her clothes. Stuffed at the very back of it was a small school tin trunk, which Posie kept her treasures in. Here was her mother's rose-gold locket with a tiny photograph of Posie and Richard cut carefully out and stuck inside on opposite sides of the hinge. Here were her photographs of Harry Briskow and her brother Richard in their uniforms just before they left for the war, and here too were letters from both, sent from the front line.

Several letters from her father were gathered here too, as well as random bits and pieces from other family and friends.

She unlocked the tin trunk and started to scrabble through its precious contents.

Was it possible? It seemed fantastical.

It was Len's stupid talking about that nurse that had done it: he had mentioned a hostel on Rupert Street, and only today she and *Chief* Inspector Lovelace had seen a couple of nurses in the Post Office there. That walk with the Inspector had seemed so unpromising at the time.

Here it was.

Posie found the sepia-coloured postcard near the bottom of her things. She read it quickly and gasped aloud.

She had been right. Here was her blackmailer. *But how could it be?*

Dulcie Deane. Back from the dead. *Another* one back from the dead.

She was skim-reading the postcard from Dulcie Deane from January 1918, which had informed Posie of the death of her crew, including Merlin the dog. In which Dulcie had invited Posie to meet her in London after the war.

Dulcie had often mentioned living at a London hostel

for nurses, but Posie had never paid much notice to her. But here now was the proof; the postcode, W1D – the postcode for Rupert Street – was given emphatically. And even more damningly, the clear, schoolgirlish hand from 1918 was *the same* as the one which had written the three Christmas cards to Felicity Fyne.

But Dulcie Deane was dead! It was a given. The Imperial War Graves Commission even had an exact place for her burial site.

Posie racked her brain. If Dr Winter had somehow come out of that annihilating bomb blast alive, why not Dulcie Deane, too? She wouldn't be the first person to fake her own death and go back to what she had loved best: London, the bright lights, the safety net of a hostel in Soho. But perhaps it hadn't worked out that well, after all. Perhaps Dulcie had gone back to a job which paid too little, and returned to a life which proved just a little too lonely, and had been fuelled by feelings of jealousy for a woman who had seemed to have had much more going for her, even if appearances could be deceptive, as Posie now knew.

But was Posie wildly wrong?

Did Dulcie – the Dulcie she had known – have it in her to blackmail someone? Surely not. But sadness and loneliness could change a person. That was true, too. And how did Dulcie know that Dr Winter was alive, anyhow? Posie chewed at her lip, sitting on her haunches, holding the years-old postcard in her hands.

She decided that she would go back to Rupert Street tomorrow, after her appointment with Professor Winter at King's Cross. She would investigate. Try and find out for certain if Dulcie Deane was living there now or not.

Posie barely noticed that Bikram had slunk in through her bedroom door and had sat companionably down at her side, his eyes mournful and sad.

'Poor old fella,' Posie said absently, stroking his silky

coat. 'Both of us are being ignored tonight, aren't we? Oh, the glamour of living with a world-famous explorer. It's not all it's cracked up to be, is it? What a funny old world!'

And Posie packed away her tin trunk quickly, as if keen not to delve further into any of her other ghosts and memories which were carefully stored there.

She had quite enough on her plate as it was already.

* * * *

Eight

The next day Posie stood, seven-thirty sharp, at the entrance to Platform 5 at King's Cross. She was clutching two steaming paper cups of black tea in her hand.

She watched the steam train from Glasgow pull in to the platform, and then about a hundred people dismounted, most looking crumpled and ashen after the long journey south.

Posie didn't need to worry about missing Professor Winter, or about not recognising him. She saw him emerge, unrumpled and pristine; black-suited with a matching homburg hat and carrying a neat overnight bag. He was a carbon copy of his son, Dr William Winter, or rather, his son had been a carbon copy of the father. She remembered Felicity Fyne's comments about how William Winter had always been incredibly smart in the past, and she saw that he had got that from his father, too. Incredibly tall, straight-backed, white-blonde in colouring and resembling a fairly terrifying streak of lightning, Professor Winter looked every inch the cold, humourless professional he was. He had on a red bow tie and wore a fresh red carnation in the lapel of his expensive black woollen coat. They were like small slashes of blood in his otherwise colourless appearance and Posie found herself wondering if the effect was intentional. She also found herself annoyingly distracted; wondering how on earth Professor Winter had managed to keep the flower from wilting in the stuffy carriage of the overnighter.

She stepped into his direct path.

'Miss Parker?' There was a raise of a shaggy grey eyebrow but nothing more friendly was offered.

'That's me, sir. Cuppa?'

The Professor took a cup from her without a word and continued walking, indicating with a subtle movement of the head that they should exit to the right, through a small emergency exit, away from the crowds off the train. He obviously knew the station well and he strode along fast, Posie almost galloping along in her smart high-heeled boots to keep up with him.

Out on the busy thoroughfare outside the station they made their way past the usual early-morning crush of newspaper sellers and beggars. The rain had stopped but the pavements were black and glistening, waiting for more rain to fall. Commuters were spilling from the station like a million shiny black ants, all clutching newspapers and briefcases and cups of tea, bound for offices and shiny wooden desks all over London, all set for the last couple of work days of the year.

There was a faintly festive feeling in the air too as ex-soldiers tried to ply their trade among the crowd, offering small cheap wooden Christmas gifts for sale on brightly-decorated trays. As Posie and Professor Winter moved off from the crowds and started to walk down the Gray's Inn Road, Posie was conscious of the silence between them, and the limited time available. She didn't know where they were going, but she guessed it must be near. As if he could read her thoughts, the Professor inclined his head a little and looked down at her.

'I'm lecturing at the Royal College of Surgeons this morning,' he said by way of explanation. 'So, we have about twenty minutes' walk to Lincoln's Inn Fields. What's this all about then?'

Posie noticed the slight Scottish burr, more like Edinburgh than Glasgow, in his voice, and she noticed how it was unlike his son's voice, which had betrayed nothing of his Scottish roots. A searing image of Dr Winter, as she had last seen him came suddenly into her mind: rising abruptly from the table on Christmas Day in 1917, the telegram about Helena's death clutched in his hand, his face unreadable.

It had not been her intention to reveal her personal connection with the case to Professor Winter, but she knew suddenly it was right. She felt sure that this tall, upright man who had granted her a precious twenty minutes of his time had the right to know what she was up to. She quickly explained her background, and outlined the unusual case so far: the likely *vanishing*, rather than the death, of Dr Winter. She mentioned Felicity Fyne and watched a cloud settle darkly across the man's face.

'I just wondered, sir,' she concluded, studying the Professor's silent, closed-up face, 'whether you or your wife had had any contact with your son these last four years, since 1918 when he was supposed to have died?'

The Professor emitted a short, sharp shrill of ironic laughter.

'You ought to be grateful, girl, that I'm used to hard knocks and shocks. What you're telling me, in other words, is that my only son, my only child, is still alive?'

Posie nodded.

'Bah, humbug! Rot! Sheer rot! I don't believe it! In my book the dead stay dead, and I should know, eh? I see enough corpses in my line of work. And you should be ashamed of yourself. Call yourself a Private Detective? Seems to me you've gone along with the ravings of a fantasist! That woman! *That Fyne woman*. She was a really bad lot. You should get hold of some real facts before you go around making sweeping statements like that. It sounds like a wee mare's nest to me, Missie.'

Posie winced. She realised a lot of what she was going on was a hunch, and she was desperately looking for a break; a lead to make this all concrete, to make connections. She hated the ring of truth in the Professor's words, so like Inspector Lovelace's comments to her on the telephone the previous day.

'I know it seems unbelievable, sir, and I'm sorry if it comes to nothing. I just wondered if there might be anything you could add which might help me find him. *If* he is still alive.'

The Professor stopped in the middle of the pavement. The rain had started up again but he didn't open an umbrella. Anger flashed in his pale blue eyes:

'My son is dead, full-stop. He was our only son, and if he had somehow lived I can guarantee he would have contacted us. Don't you think so? He was his mother's pride and joy, and she lived for him. He knew that very well. *Lived* for him, understand me?'

Posie swallowed. *You lived for him too*, she thought to herself sadly. But she didn't like the Professor's use of the past tense when speaking about his wife. She nodded mutely, slicking her wet hair out of her eyes.

'My wife Morag collapsed when we received the telegram about William's death.'

Posie nodded again, remembering it was almost exactly the same thing that had happened to her own father on learning of Richard's death. She held her tongue though. They started to walk again, the rain now slapping the pavement. The oily tarry smell of the wet tarmac filled their nostrils, that unmistakeable scent of London. A smart wind was getting up again. The Professor resumed.

'But Morag would probably still be here today if we hadn't received *another* letter, a month later. We received a wee letter from this upstart; this good-for-nothing girl, Felicity Fyne.'

Posie frowned, not understanding the malice behind the words. Many would have agreed with the Professor about Felicity but only *after* having met her, so what exactly lay behind the hatred?

'That letter from Felicity Fyne caused my wife to suffer a fatal heart attack,' the Professor continued, negotiating a crowd of barristers coming out of Gray's Inn, holding onto their wigs and gowns for dear life. 'She practically caused my wife's death.'

'I'm so very sorry.'

'Don't be. It's not your fault, and I'm not asking for your sympathy. It was probably for the best. Morag wouldn't have wanted to go on living anyway without William. It wasn't as if there were even any children as a result of the marriage. Or *were* there, do you know?'

A keen intense light shone for a split-second in his eyes, then died when Posie shook her head firmly. Professor Winter looked away quickly and continued:

'You see, as I said, William was Morag's whole life. It was all right for me: I had, and still have, my work.'

Your work. And an empty, aching heart within that straight-backed exterior, Posie thought to herself. She felt an unexpected stab of pity for the man next to her, but she forced herself to be logical; to shake off the sentiment which was beginning to weigh on her heavily.

'I don't understand, sir,' she questioned in as professional a manner as she could muster. 'What *exactly* was your problem with Felicity Fyne, sir? What did she say to you that was so shocking?'

Again the ironic laughter. They took a sharp right onto High Holborn.

'The fact William had got married to the woman at all was a huge shock. It was news to us. He hadn't bothered to inform us. Here we were with a daughter-in-law.'

'Well, sir, I think it all happened in a bit of a rush...' Posie hazarded guardedly. 'There might not have been much time to tell you. Your son was working in very demanding conditions. Maybe he didn't have time to write to you?'

'Rot!' spat the Professor. 'He wrote every week to his mother, without fail. He'd written to his mother the day before his death. Never mentioned this woman once, let alone that he'd bally well gone and married her! And don't talk balderdash – of course he had time to break the news; they'd been married at least a couple of months when he died.'

Posie winced. 'I don't know why that was, then, sir. I can only imagine your shock.'

'Oh, I *know* why he didn't mention it, all right,' said the Professor acidly. They were drawing close to Chancery Lane and they took a shortcut through the law court gardens, empty but for a few black-suited men sheltering under large, precarious looking umbrellas.

'That woman, that flibbertigibbet, Felicity Fyne, she sent a photograph of herself and William together on their wedding day, as if to prove it to us, I suppose. Smugness itself. So we'd believe that the marriage had actually happened.'

'Was that so bad? Perhaps she was just trying to make a connection with you? I'm no friend of the woman, I can assure you, but she seems genuinely broken by William's death. *If* he has died.'

'More likely she was after our money. But that wasn't the problem. It was what she *looked* like that brought back terrible memories.'

'Oh? I don't quite follow.'

They were passing under the big terracotta brick arch of Lincoln's Inn and out into the sodden square of Lincoln's Inn Fields. Outside the grand Grecian-columned building of the Royal College of Surgeons they came to an abrupt stop.

The Professor looked intently down at Posie. Something changed in his expression and the steely cold resolve seemed to melt a little before her eyes. *He's going to tell me something important*, Posie thought to herself. *Something he's hardly told anyone.* She willed him to go on. She nodded encouragingly.

'Look here, I feel I can trust you for some reason. But you mustn't break my confidence in what I'm about to tell you, Miss Parker. These are private family matters. Understand?'

Posie nodded again. She had this effect on people sometimes; they felt they could spill the beans on all sorts of things without any consequences, which was jolly handy in her line of work.

'As you know, my son was a skilled surgeon, and he was making quite a name for himself before the war.'

You were proud of him, you mean, thought Posie. *Why can't you just say it?*

'But he had a weakness.'

Posie stared. She couldn't imagine what the man was talking about. The Dr Winter she had known had seemed like control itself. What secret demons had he harboured? Was it drink? Drugs? Gambling on the dogs or horses?

Professor Winter sighed.

'I'll be candid with you. My son was a frightful womaniser. He had a weakness for women. All the same type. Particularly *beautiful* women.' And here he half-glanced at Posie through lowered eyelids, as if just checking to make certain he couldn't include her in that dangerous category. Evidently satisfied, he continued:

'When he was eighteen my son met a woman, a wee actress. It changed his life, changed *him*. He met her when she was playing the lead role, Perdita, in *The Winter's Tale*. It was in Glasgow, at the Theatre Royal, and she was a real piece of work. Beautiful, but common as muck, and she lived in a very fast manner, if you get my drift. She dragged William into all kinds of trouble. He was going to elope with her to Gretna Green – imagine – *my* son, with an actress! I stopped them just in time. I broke it up. It would have ruined him. He'd never have gone off to Cambridge. Imagine…'

The Professor looked over at the shiny wet steps under the big portico of the Royal College where several men were now gathering. Posie read regret and suffering in his pale tired eyes.

'Well, of course, because of the play's title, William thought it was "meant to be" or some such rot. I managed to pack him off to university just in time and threatened to cut off his allowance if he didn't go but when he came back for Christmas that first year he was still determined to marry the bally woman. His mind was made up. But fortunately she'd disappeared. Vanished into thin air. Thank goodness! *The Winter's Tale* had finished its run, of course. But William lost his head over it. Blamed me. Went a bit potty. Threatened me with a gun once, too, which I never told his mother about of course. Underneath that cool calm exterior of his I wondered just what sort of a son I had sired. To be honest it drove a big rift between us. He never forgave me for his loss. My son and I were always somewhat estranged after that debacle. More's the pity.'

The Professor was staring into the distance, beyond the here and now. He suddenly regained his grip on the present:

'He never forgot her. In fact, he carried a copy of *The Winter's Tale* with him forever after. He always was mad keen on literature – Shakespeare, the lot – if I'd left it to him that's what he would have studied at university; not medicine. People think he followed me into the profession willingly, but it wasn't the case at the time. He continued to love the theatre. It was a passion. Always went to a show when he got the chance, both in London and Cambridge…'

'I'm frightfully sorry, but I don't quite see, sir…'

'He spent the rest of his time at university studying, but

really he was mooning after this actress, Perdita. For seven years. Always looking for her, putting advertisements into the papers; enquiring on the theatre circuits. But he never found her. She must have gone to the bad, or else died. Well, when we got that letter and photograph from Felicity Fyne after William had died, it was like seeing a ghost. There she was! The spitting image of this wretched Perdita whom I had spent all that time prising him away from! In fact, I thought it *was* her at first. Of course William wouldn't have wanted me to see that photograph, or to ever meet Felicity. It was obvious that he had only married her because of the very close similarity to the actress.'

'Golly! How unfortunate. I see.'

'Morag and I had a huge row about that ruddy letter and that photograph. Dredged up the past; all my dealings with William over that actress. Morag felt I'd been too harsh on the lad. Even suggested we meet this Felicity girl! Worked herself up into a right old state when I said no, and then, well… I've told you what happened.'

So you caused your wife's death, thought Posie. *It wasn't Felicity at all.*

'Tell me,' said the Professor, a note of real interest in his voice, 'I can imagine that William was almost beside himself when he first encountered Felicity Fyne, wasn't he? He must have thought it was all his Christmases come at once! Perdita, restored to him. I bet he couldn't wait to get married to Miss Fyne, huh?'

'You could say he was in a bit of a rush, sir. Yes.'

'I've got to go. My colleagues up there are waiting for me,' the Professor nodded towards the crowd on the steps, almost reluctantly. He frowned a little. 'Perhaps I've said too much. Forgive me. I don't get the chance to talk too much about my son nowadays. Was there anything else you wanted from me, Miss Parker?'

Posie bit her lip. The rain was turning to sleet and her face felt numb in the chill wind. She was desperately trying to think of anything Professor Winter might know which could help her to find his son.

'Do you happen to know if your son had any nicknames at school or university? Any names he was known by affectionately? Something he could be using as a pseudonym?'

The blank stare Professor Winter gave her answered her question more than adequately.

'Oh, one last thing. Do you remember if William ever mentioned a Helena Llewellyn to you? She worked with him at the Casualty Clearing Station in Arras, too. She was a Sister there.'

A faint flash of recognition passed across the Professor's face for a second.

'Ah! Aye. William *did* write to us about her. Told us he was engaged to be married to the lass. Sent a photograph too. Nice big fat lassie, wasn't she? Dark? Sensible sort. Seemed he'd acted wisely for once, seen sense at last; realised that looks aren't everything. Morag and I were delighted at the news. Goodness, I'd forgotten all about the fat lassie. What happened to her? I take it she died or something and then William met this woman who looked like Perdita?'

'Something like that sir, yes.' There was no point in shattering what little illusion Professor Winter retained of his son's conduct with women. Some things were better left unsaid.

'Take my advice, Miss Parker. Leave this well alone. You're wasting your time. And mine. As I said, these are the delusions of a fantasist. There's nothing worse. I bet this Felicity Fyne won't even pay your fee.'

Posie watched the famous surgeon walk away without a second glance behind him. She found herself strangely moved by him in a way she had never expected to.

I will find your son for you, if indeed he is still alive, she thought to herself as she watched the Professor striding up the steps with his strange lurching walk.

And then she walked back around the gardens of Lincoln's Inn Fields, under the rain-drenched oaks, only half-seeing a pony and trap parked at the corner of the square, where a long queue of beggars had assembled, waiting for a cup of coffee and a bowl of porridge. She had forgotten that the park was famous for hosting a soup kitchen in wintertime, and that beggars from across central London flocked there in the hopes of some refreshment; something to keep out the cold. Most of the men looked bedraggled and damp, and some turned their faces towards Posie, expressing brief flickers of hopeful interest, detecting a woman with a bit of money.

And Posie looked back intently, scanning the dirty faces with an almost anxious panic, whereas normally she would have scuttled onwards somewhat shamefully, guilty that her lot in life was so much better than theirs.

You could be here, Dr Winter, she thought to herself. *Right under our noses, and just a stone's throw away from your father. You could have been here all along. One of these poor wretches, living a life you were not born to.*

But then she chided herself for her ludicrous flight of fancy. London was so full of the poor and people shirking their own shadows right now that to find one single soul amongst the masses would be nothing short of a miracle.

But it seemed that that was exactly what she needed.

* * * *

Nine

When she got back to the Grape Street Bureau, Posie found a hive of early-morning activity, albeit that the clock had not yet struck nine. All the lights were on and the fire was already lit. More Christmas cards had arrived with the first post and they were sitting neatly stacked, waiting for Prudence's attentions in stringing them up around the room.

Peeling off her horrible wet layers she noticed that Mr Minks had taken the prime spot by the fire in the waiting room. He ignored her imperiously as she hung up her gloves and scarf and hat on the brass fender to dry. The room held the bitter tang of coffee which had been left on the Primus stove too long, the scent wafting through from the kitchen. Prudence never could quite get the hang of coffee, somehow.

Len was on the telephone speaking to a lawyer client in very loud, very grand, very important tones. He was simultaneously ripping apart a piece of red tinsel which had previously festooned the front of Prudence's desk. He seemed very out of sorts. Posie soon realised why. Alaric was in the office too, and there was no love lost between the two men.

Alaric was standing next to Prudence's desk with his

hands full of handwritten notes and a mouthful of paper-clips. He had pushed his linen shirtsleeves high above his elbows and his trousers looked like they were held up with a length of fraying string. His posture was of one at a time of high crisis.

'Prudence, were there any messages from Inspector Lovelace or any of his men for me? Or from anyone else, for that matter?'

Prudence shook her head but didn't look up.

Prudence was bashing away at her black Underwood typewriter as if her life depended on it, a dark-red flush stealing unattractively across her neck and face. Occasionally she would nod her head, and Posie saw that Alaric was dictating something to her at breakneck speed. It wasn't altogether surprising that Alaric had managed to get Prudence to moonlight for him. Prudence had a thing for handsome men. In addition to her penchant for titles, she was also rather attracted to famous people. In Alaric, formerly Lord Boynton-Dale, she had got all three.

Alaric was one of the aristocratic Boynton-Dale family, a family besmirched by an unenviable notoriety, which he hated and did his best to ignore. He was also very famous in his own right, and his exploits as an explorer were often in the daily newspapers and penny magazines. As a result Prudence almost worshipped the ground he walked on. Annoyingly.

Posie clucked her tongue loudly:

'Is that your talk for tomorrow which you're getting poor Prudence to type up, Al? She's rather busy with the work I *pay* her to do, you know.'

'Mnnnn? I'm sorry, darling. It won't take more than five of her precious minutes. I promise.'

Alaric gave Posie a peck on the cheek and smiled his lopsided, lovely smile and his strange copper-coloured eyes twinkled in the bright electric light. Posie rolled her eyes heavenwards and mumbled something audibly about *ships which pass in the night.* Which Alaric may or may not have heard. He certainly didn't bother to respond, either way.

Len came off the telephone and glared around malevolently before shuffling off to his own office, tea cup in hand and his morning post stuffed under his arm. Posie was just studying her own parcel of post when the office telephone rang again. She snatched it up and the Operator asked if she would accept a call from the Board of Education in Whitehall, from a Constable Smallpenny.

The policeman was transferred through after a short wait.

'Miss Parker? I'm working for Chief Inspector Lovelace on this project of yours.'

Posie tried to sound calm and collected. 'Ah, yes. Have you found anything for me?'

'No,' the voice came back resolutely. 'Two of us were here last night for an hour and Constable Phillips and myself have been here since early this morning. We've been through every possibility there is. We checked against the name "Winter" and all derivations of "Winter" for all the Schoolmasters who started teaching in private schools in England since the Great War, from 1918 up to now. We've checked your fella's date of birth against every single man appointed to teach a science subject, too, just in case we missed him somehow, but there isn't anyone who seems to match the man you're looking for, even allowing for discrepancies with the date of birth.'

Posie blew out a great breath. She hadn't realised quite how much she had been staking on this little investigation, hoping it would throw up a clue, a lead. Now she had nothing. No idea where to turn next. Perhaps she had been wrong to follow her hunch about Dr Winter having become a Schoolmaster, after all? Perhaps, as Professor Winter believed, William Winter really was dead.

'Thank you, Constable. You've been very thorough. Were there an awful lot of new Schoolmasters? A lot of men starting to teach the sciences since the war?'

'Yes, a good couple of hundred. Some men re-entering the profession and others starting from scratch having left the armed services.'

'Well, thank you for your time, Constable. I do appreciate it. I'm sorry it was a dead end.'

A small embarrassed-sounding cough came down the line:

'I say, Miss Parker. Constable Phillips and I are here now. The weather's lousy outside. We've been given leave by the Chief Inspector to stay here until noon if necessary on this project for you. We're more than happy to stay and search some more. In fact, we've got all the indexes of the schools out right now in front of us. Do you have any other leads? Any other names we can search for? Any other subjects your man might be teaching? Any other possibilities, however random, which might throw up your fella?'

Posie's mind was a total blank. She couldn't think of a single thing. She said so.

'Tell you what,' said Constable Smallpenny, who was clearly in no rush to return to New Scotland Yard and was enjoying his relatively 'free' morning, 'you think on it, Miss Parker. We'll stay on here another hour, until ten. If something comes to you, telephone us here.'

Posie hung up the receiver, feeling crushed. The words *'mare's nest'* kept floating through her mind, and she had absolutely no new ideas. Just then the telephone rang again.

Sighing, Posie picked it up and the Operator asked if she would accept a call from the Post Office in Hampstead Village, London NW3.

'Oh, go on then,' she said crossly, which she immediately regretted. It wasn't the Operator's fault that her morning had been unfruitful. She had got precisely nowhere. While she was waiting for the call to be put through she grabbed her notebook and turned to the hasty note she had made about her meeting that morning with Professor Winter.

Was there anything there which might help her now?

'Posie?' It was Felicity Fyne. The last person she felt like talking to. There was, after all, nothing concrete to report. Nothing at all, in fact.

'I'm glad I caught you. I don't have a telephone in my shop. So I walked here. Just wondering if there was any news yet?'

Posie's instinctive irritation was blunted by the sound of suppressed desperation in the woman's voice on the other end of the line.

'No, I'm frightfully sorry but I don't have anything definite yet. I'm pursuing several leads, but so far they've come to nothing.'

'*Oh.*'

'Actually, I met your husband's father this morning. It was interesting, but not very illuminating, I'm afraid.'

Posie didn't know why she said it, for it went against her normal rule of not talking about progress with clients until a case was solved, but something had to give. Besides, there was a chance that Felicity might actually know something useful.

There was a small silence. Posie flicked her notebook.

'What was he like?'

'Oh, as you described. A cold fish, really. Although he obviously misses his son. His wife died.' Posie omitted to say how, or why, or to mention the role of Felicity's letter in the sorry tale.

'I wondered…It's probably nothing, but did your husband have any nicknames, or any aliases he might have used, ever?'

'Sorry? No, no. I'm certain of it.'

'Anything he was really fond of? Any especial pets he spoke about? Any sports he played? Any special tobacco he smoked? Anything? Anything at all?'

At the deafening silence from the other end of the line Posie continued, remembering what Professor Winter had told her about his son's passion for the theatre.

'The theatre? A favourite book? Any particular literature? Any interests outside of medicine, I mean.'

'No. None that I know of. He was just dedicated to his
work. That was his whole life.'

Posie caught her breath and blew outwards in disbelief.
So Dr Winter hadn't even shared his love of theatre and
literature with Felicity Fyne. Had she really known the
man she had so hastily married at all? What on earth had
they spoken of to each other? If they had spoken at all,
that was.

'Okay. Well, thanks anyway. I'll get back to you by
Saturday. Then you can decide which colour hats to put
out in time for Christmas Eve.'

Posie checked her wristwatch quickly, it was quarter-to
ten. She threw caution to the wind in her desperation.

'You didn't know Dulcie Deane well, did you, in Arras?
Do you remember her? She was a regular nursing Sister.'

'Who?'

Posie described Dulcie as best she could. Dyed hair,
freckly, prone to gossip, forgettable. She could practically
hear the cogs whirring in Felicity's mind.

'Oh! Yes. *That* little nobody.'

Posie counted to five and tried to remember that she
wasn't duty bound to *like* her clients.

'But she's dead!' resumed Felicity, unfeelingly. 'Why are
you asking me about *her*?'

Why indeed, Posie asked herself miserably. *In for a penny,
in for a pound.*

'No reason. It was just a line of enquiry which didn't
lead very far.'

She cast her eyes over her notebook hurriedly, she saw
the last line from her meeting with Professor Winter. The
name "Perdita" scrawled there haphazardly.

'And "Perdita"? Does that mean anything to you?'

Posie could hear a shudderingly sharp intake of breath
down the line.

'Does it? If you know anything, please tell me.'

After a slight pause, Felicity said in a much smaller voice than before:

'No, "Perdita" doesn't mean anything to *me*. But it obviously did to William. When he died I had to collect all of his personal belongings from his tent, as I told you. Well, there wasn't much. But there was one book, a play, *The Winter's Tale*. I'd seen him reading it sometimes at night. It seemed to calm him down. It was really dog-eared and looked like it had been everywhere with him. I've thrown it out since. On the flyleaf were the words "*To my opposite number, my other half. My darling Flo. From Perdita. I love you until the end.*" It's burned into my mind, word for word. There was a date, too. Sometime around the end of the last century.'

'What? Can you repeat that? I'll write it down.'

'Why? How can *that* be useful?'

'I'm not sure it is. But this is the second time I'm hearing this woman's name mentioned, and you never know.'

Felicity repeated the memorised inscription with an ill grace. 'I have to say, it made me feel pretty horrible, reading that after he had died. Cheap. As if he was still in love with whoever Perdita was. It was a shock. *I* was supposed to be the love of his life.'

Posie gulped. 'I'm sorry to be dredging up bad memories for you. I'll come back to you soon. I promise.'

Posie rang off. She stared into space. She was vaguely aware of Alaric clipping pages together in the corner of the room like a madman. She didn't realise he was looking at her with some concern.

'What is it, love?' Alaric said in his low, enchanting, gravelly voice, cutting in on her train of thought.

'Oh, nothing,' she snapped irritably, looking at her wristwatch again. Her time, or rather Constable Smallpenny's time, was almost up.

A thought suddenly came to her. A wild, crazy, urgent thought.

Her memories of the past and her judgements about people she had known back then were proving to be fairly distorted, and even plain wrong on occasion. She had assumed that Dr Winter was solely focussed on his medical career; that he didn't have an artistic or imaginative bone in his body. How wrong she had been! So perhaps she had been very wrong too in instructing Chief Inspector Lovelace's men to search only for a limited range of pseudonyms at the Board of Education. It seemed Dr Winter was capable of much, much more than she had given him credit for.

'Where's the nearest Public Library to here which would be open right now, just a couple of days before Christmas?'

'Theobald's Road,' Prudence said automatically, without looking up from her final adjustments to Alaric's talk. 'I go there twice a week. I know the opening hours like the back of my hand.'

Alaric raised a quizzical eyebrow: books and literature were not really his thing, which was quite ironic really as he lived comfortably off the income from book royalties; the books of a cousin of his who had died and assigned him all of her rights in her Will.

'What is it that you need? I can get it tonight for you?' Prudence offered. She patted her unfashionably long hair back into its hairnet and adjusted her spectacles, keen to curry favour while Alaric was still in the room.

'That's too late,' Posie said, grimacing and heading to the fender to retrieve her damp outdoor clothes. 'I need Shakespeare's "*Collected Works*"! And I need it now.'

'What is it you want to know?' asked Alaric, casually. He picked up Posie's notebook and read what she had written there. The last page.

'Perdita? From *The Winter's Tale*?' he asked. His gorgeous eyes shimmered at her.

'That's the one.'

'"*To my opposite number, my other half. My darling Flo.*" Well, I know that Perdita's opposite number in the play is Florizel. I take it that's the "Flo" mentioned here?'

Posie gasped, gobsmacked: 'How on earth do you know *that*? I thought you didn't read, let alone Shakespeare!'

'Posh school,' Alaric said, slightly embarrassed. He was shuffling his newly-typed talk into a manila folder and was struggling into his battered Burberry raincoat and belting it up all at the same time. 'We had to read all the plays. In fact, *The Winter's Tale* is one of the clearest which remains in my addled memory.'

'Oh? Why's that, Mr Boynton-Dale?' asked Prudence, all agog for his answer.

Posie had lurched towards the telephone and was already placing a call with the Operator, but she listened intently to Alaric's reply.

'Oh, well, the story is memorable in its own way. The enduring memory you're left with is of one of the main characters who's supposedly died, but actually it turns out they've been alive all along, just in hiding. Hiding under everyone's noses. They just did a good job of vanishing. That's all.'

Posie was staring at Alaric in absolute disbelief. *It fitted! It all fitted!* He mouthed a quick 'goodbye' at her and then headed off.

She clasped the collar of her navy woollen jumper nervously. A deep crackling voice could be heard coming on the line.

'Constable Smallpenny? Posie Parker here again. I'm so glad I caught you. Just one last name to check, if that's okay? Yes. Yes, I'll wait. It's a bit unusual, I'll grant you that.'

A couple of seconds later there was more crackling. A pen had been found.

'Florizel. Check that out. Are any new Schoolmasters

called Florizel? Yes, of course. I'll spell it out. F-L-O-R-I-Z-E-L. Yes. I'll wait for your call back.'

* * * *

As she waited, Posie studied her nails carefully, so as not to think about the rising tides of butterflies which were fluttering around in her stomach.

Posie Parker was a marketing man's dream: a sucker for anything which spoke of hot climes and exotic escapes, she consequently had an enviable nail varnish collection of garish shades with names such as 'Riviera' or 'Tropical Beach'. Today she had on 'Watermelon', a hot pink shade by Maybelline which had looked rather wonderful in the window of the Army & Navy Store on Victoria Street back in the summer but now in the December gloom of the office made Posie's hands look an unfortunate shade of green. She chewed a nail and felt a bit of the Watermelon colour flaking off.

The desk clock struck ten and Len slunk out from his office, cup in hand. Prudence collected the mugs and stood to make the tea; she had taken it on as her sole responsibility when she started at the Grape Street Bureau and now couldn't be swayed from the idea of this being one of her key duties, despite the very weak 'filth' which she managed to brew, and the not infrequent complaints she received.

'I'll have a proper cuppa today, Pru,' said Len cheekily, his spirits much restored by finding Alaric gone. 'None of this "kiss of tea" lark. I want a nice sugary brown cuppa which I can stand my spoon up in. Builder's tea. Otherwise, I'll make it myself.'

Prudence left the room muttering darkly to herself and Posie continued to eye the telephone, willing it to ring.

'I'll have my cuppa and be off,' said Len conversation-ally. 'I've got a case on in the West End today. I'm supposed to be catching a famous actress taking more than a curtain call with her leading man; her husband's not best pleased, as you can imagine, and wants to press for a divorce. So yours truly is after some top-notch photographs to help him on his way.'

Posie grimaced. A lot of Len's 'shadowing' work left her cold; it was often murky stuff but it paid a good deal of their bills at the Grape Street Bureau, so it wasn't her place to come over all sensitive about it.

'You off out anywhere yourself, Po?' Len shifted his weight from foot to foot in the doorway.

'As it happens, I am. I'm off to Rupert Street again. To your nurses' hostel, actually. Do you remember where it was, exactly?'

But just then the telephone rang and Prudence appeared simultaneously with the tea tray and a packet of Peek Frean's Golden Puffs. What Len was saying by way of reply was swallowed up in the excitement of the news from the Home Office:

'You were spot on, Miss Parker! We've got him!' Constable Smallpenny made it sound as if they had just located a seasoned arch criminal who had been on the run forever, rather than a distinguished surgeon who had gone into hiding for what might turn out to be the very best of reasons, but Posie was too excited to care.

'Your Mr Florizel started to work at the Wickham Academy for Boys at Bishop's Stortford in the summer of 1918. Almost the real date of birth was given, too. Just a couple of days out, it was.'

'Thank you. Thank you so much. Golly! That's ace.'

'You were wrong through, Miss, about one thing. He's not teaching any science subject. It's English Literature he's teaching. Does that fit at all?'

* * * *

Posie came off the phone in a state of high excitement. Len had gone already so it was only Prudence left, much deflated by finding herself alone with just Posie for company.

'I have him! I have him!' Posie announced gleefully to no one in particular.

Posie suddenly remembered her meeting the next day with Mrs Greenwood outside King's College in Cambridge.

'Bishop's Stortford? That's near Cambridge, isn't it, Prudence? I need to get there, tomorrow if possible.'

'Yes,' said Prudence, nodding, getting out a copy of *The ABC Railway Guide* from her top drawer. She thumbed through it until she found the right page.

'You're due at two o'clock tomorrow in Cambridge, aren't you? I looked in your desk diary. You could easily do both things in one day. Those two places are on the same train route.'

Posie nodded, marvelling as usual at how efficient, or how nosy, her secretary really was.

'You could take a train to Bishop's Stortford in the morning, say for eleven. Then pick up a connecting train to Cambridge at one o'clock when you've finished. You'll get to Cambridge in plenty of time for your appointment. Then, later, when you've finished in Cambridge, you can get a direct train back to London and be home in time for tea.'

Posie found herself nodding along dumbly. She asked Prudence to arrange the tickets, and then to call Wickham Academy to arrange a meeting with the Headmaster and also with Mr Florizel. She told Prudence to pretend that she, Posie, was a parent; anxious to visit the school to see if it might be a prospective place for her son.

'It's already the Christmas holidays for schools. So I need a legitimate excuse to turn up tomorrow, spying. Pretend to be my personal assistant. Tell them that I'm a rich mother whose son has a particular interest in English Literature and I wish to speak to a Schoolmaster who specialises in it, to see if it might be a suitable place.'

Prudence flushed. She wasn't entirely in her comfort zone, lying. It didn't come naturally to her.

'What name shall I give for your son?' she asked, a little stiffly. 'They're bound to ask.'

Posie used the first name which came into her mind. For some reason she thought again of Evangeline Greenwood and the strange business with the unanswered letter last year, and now the strange invite to goodness-only-knew-what in Cambridge tomorrow.

'Tell them the boy is called Harry Eden,' she said without much hesitation.

'That name is etched on my brain for some reason already. At least I know I won't forget it. Now I've got to dash. I'm off to visit one of Len's old haunts. Wish me luck.'

* * * *

Ten

Posie walked up and down Rupert Street several times in the pouring rain, but couldn't find a hostel of any kind anywhere. The rain seemed to have set in for the day and was lashing down in stinging sheets. Dozens of black umbrellas thronged the pavements, obscuring the identities of the people they covered, making going along difficult.

Eventually she gave up and sought shelter in the same Post Office she had visited just the day before with Inspector Lovelace. Standing shivering by a display of writing papers, she watched the rain continue to fall.

Just then a petite, elfin girl entered the building, clutching at a grey waterproof cape which seemed much too large for her tiny frame. When she shook out the hood, Posie saw that the girl was wearing the familiar white hood and cap of a professional nurse underneath.

'I say,' Posie said, darting over and coming straight to the point. 'I'm frightfully sorry but can you help me? I'm lost. Is there a nurses' hostel in this street at all? It's just that I'm supposed to be meeting a friend there for coffee, and I thought it would be easy to find, but I can't find it at all!'

The girl laughed merrily:

'Don't worry. Lots of people have difficulties finding it!

I live there, I should know. It's number 53B, on the same side of the road as this, about halfway down. The reason you can't find it is because the original hostel was bombed in the Great War; all that's left is a great crater in the ground. They've built a new hostel on the site next door to the original, but there's no plaque or name up yet, even though it's been standing almost four years now. The builders are taking a positive age finishing it off: there are still wooden hoardings all around it and it looks scruffy from the outside. Inside it's not yet finished either, but beggars can't be choosers. Still, most nurses would give their eye-teeth for a room in the Rupert Street hostel.'

Posie nodded. She remembered Dulcie had loved living there before the war. It was about as central as you could get.

'How do you go about getting a room then?'

'Priority was given to those who had had a room in the previous hostel, before the bombing. After that there was a waiting list as long as your arm for the other rooms.' The elfin girl beamed at Posie, happy with her lot in life.

'Still, it was worth the wait; I love living here. I hope you meet your friend.'

Somehow, if Posie's crazy theory was correct, it would seem that Dulcie might have been one of those lucky few from the old hostel who had managed to keep the right to a room in the new one.

No wonder Len hadn't found his girl, Posie thought to herself uncharitably. If the place had been bombed to oblivion who knew what chaos and uncertainties had followed? It was the same old story of people losing contact, losing touch. Posie felt a slight twinge of guilt: she had been so cross hearing about Len's nurse-girlfriend that she hadn't bothered to listen to the end of Len's story about his search for the woman at all. In fact, she didn't think she's let him even explain that there had been a bomb dropped on the place, which might have saved her some time.

Posie found the hostel, and was glad she had asked someone in the know. Number 53B was obscured by damp chipboard hoardings, and bill posters had been pasted up everywhere, now going soggy in the rain. Next door was a huge hole in the ground, as large as an ocean liner, with rubble splayed everywhere. Edging her way through a rough wooden door cut into the hoardings, Posie found herself at the foot of some brick steps, in front of a new red-brick building in the current art deco style. She was apprehensive: what if she saw Dulcie Deane right away? Would she just confront her openly and have done with it?

Inside, there was a small reception area with a sideboard for magazines and a jug of water and lemon, and a small warden's office. The place smelt of a curious mix of antiseptic and sawdust, and a small fake Christmas tree had been placed just inside the front door on a pristine linoleum floor. Packets of Christmas cards were on sale at the warden's counter.

'You don't belong here, do you, Missy?' A booming voice came from the warden's office.

'Can I help you?'

Its tones suggested the owner of the voice would rather do anything *but* help Posie. The owner turned out to be a very fat woman in her late fifties, large and ponderous in a black oilcloth overall, who sat beside a wall-eyed man who was busy reading a newspaper. They were obviously a married couple and each bore a strange familiar resemblance to the other, as is often the case when people have been married a very long time.

Posie tried her most enchanting smile.

'Actually, you might be able to help me, thank you for asking. I'm looking for a friend of mine. We worked together during the Great War, in Arras. She told me to look her up here and that's just what I'm doing.'

The fat woman curled her lip, unimpressed:

'The war finished a good while ago now, Missy. Or

didn't anyone tell you? You've left it a bit late to get pally now, haven't you?'

Posie saw the woman's point and smiled again. A small white lie seemed like it might be necessary and she explained as convincingly as possible that she had been abroad for some years, in India, and was only just back. That she was only just now picking up where she had left off.

The warden stared back, unconvinced. Then at last she took out a register with a pen fixed to it with a piece of dirty string.

'Name of the nurse you wish to visit?'

'Dorothy Deane,' said Posie quickly before she lost her nerve, the butterflies rising uncontrollably in her stomach. 'But she was known to us all in the medical unit as Dulcie.'

Was she crazy standing here asking after a dead girl?

An ugly smile split the fat woman's face. 'Ah, why didn't you say so sooner, dearie? Dulcie is top-drawer; one of the old crew, from *before*. Smashing girl. A real lady, she is.'

She had been right! She had been right!

Posie felt like dancing a jig right there and then on the new linoleum floor.

For the first time the silent, wall-eyed man in the warden's office looked up. He was guzzling down something from a small box. Whatever it was he was eating smelt familiar to Posie; it had a strong sweet scent which carried across the counter. It smelt like something comforting from the nursery; something her nanny would have made, perhaps. He smiled. 'Aye. Dulcie is a real lady. Treats us all like Kings, she does. Works her fingers to the bone, too.'

The man's voice was surprisingly lyrical for such an ugly man.

'Oh?' said Posie, trying to remember if Dulcie had always been that hard working, or that courteous, but in truth she couldn't remember. It was too long ago, and she hadn't been that memorable. 'Yes, well. I wonder, is she in just now?'

The woman looked in another book which seemed to be a signing-in and signing-out book for nurses. She shook her head mournfully.

'I'm sorry but she's out just now,' the warden said knowingly. 'Works all hours of the day and night, she does. Do you want to leave a note?'

'Where is it she works just now?' asked Posie, avoiding the question. She absolutely *didn't* want to leave a note.

'Oh, all over London, dearie,' said the woman. 'She works for an agency, temping: takes whatever she can get, does our Dulcie. Old people's homes, or shelters, or the town hospitals when they've got a spare shift going. She's even Matron at a school nearby when the Matron-in-residence goes off sick.'

So Dulcie didn't have one main job. Strange. Why was that? It sounded like she was seriously hard up to be working so much. But did money and the need for it alone turn someone into a blackmailer?

'Shall I take a message for you, pet?' asked the woman, kindness itself. 'What was your name again?'

Posie hadn't given her name on purpose and she ignored the question now.

'Oh golly, please don't worry about it. I'll drop by again soon,' said Posie. She made a show of tidying her damp hair and rain-smudged make-up in her small silver compact mirror before leaving.

'And I'll send Dulcie a Christmas card with my details on it. Good day. And Merry Christmas to you both, too.'

Posie had her proof now. That Dulcie was still here. Now all she needed was to go away and think about how best to proceed.

As she swung out of the lobby and almost collided with a few nurses coming in on their lunch breaks, she realised that she had seen the Christmas cards at the counter before: cheap and gaudy with just a smudge of green glitter, they had been the exact same ones that had been sent with the blackmailing messages to Felicity Fyne, three years running.

Posie shook her head as she stepped into the rain. *So much still didn't make sense.*

But she had the rest of the day to play with, and no appointments now until her jaunt to Cambridge tomorrow.

There was nothing more to do for Felicity Fyne other than think and hope that the puzzle pieces would come together somehow. In any case, the weather looked like it would stay foul, and nearby was Regent Street and the alluring delights of the Burlington Arcade.

But first, lunch was in order. And the Florence Restaurant was so temptingly close.

* * * *

PART THREE
Friday 22nd December, 1922

Eleven

The Headmaster's study at Wickham Academy was cosy to the point of being suffocating. It was boiling hot, too. Posie peeled her gloves off slightly nervously.

As she sat waiting in a burnished leather armchair facing the huge old desk, she cast her eye around the room. She was used to traditional institutions, but this place took things one step further.

The blazing fire was surrounded by dark oak panelling, and the walls around were covered wall-to-ceiling with green tooled-leather books, so immaculate that Posie doubted very much that a single copy had ever been lifted from the shelves. Christmas cards dangled from a thin line of string around the wainscoting, and wherever there was a space on the walls, a black-and-white photograph of a cricket team from days long gone had been hung. The place felt claustrophobic. An old dog slumbered fitfully on an oriental red carpet. It niffed a bit, too; like a soggy woollen pullover.

Outside, although it was already eleven o'clock, the morning hadn't bothered to get light, and sheets of unforgiving grey rain slapped hard against the mullioned window pane.

'I'm sorry to keep you, Mrs Eden,' said the Headmaster

apologetically, crossing the room with his hands full of papers. The Headmaster, whose name was Doge, shuffled around his desk in his big black academic gown and sat down opposite Posie. He put his paperwork down in front of him and moved a huge glass paperweight which was filled with some unfortunate and long-dead creature which may or may not have been a shrimp. Mr Doge was a small man with a worried expression and his gown swamped him completely.

'I take it you had a good journey here and a satisfactory tour around the school, Mrs Eden?' said the Headmaster with a look of real concern in his eyes. Mr Doge was obviously someone for whom his job and his boys were his whole life, and for a second Posie felt terrible about lying: for inventing a son who quite simply didn't exist; for wasting this man's time.

'It *is* the Christmas holidays, of course. So we're just left with a few boys here, those who will stay here over Christmas. Those whose parents are too far away to collect them, diplomat's sons and the like. If it was term-time you would have got a completely different picture of the place; I could have arranged for our Head Boy to take you around, but *he's* obviously gone home for the festive season. It probably wasn't entirely satisfactory…'

Posie smiled and assured him that everything had been eminently satisfactory.

'And I'm not quite sure what the hurry was, Mrs Eden. It's not in my notes here. Why does your boy need to come to us so urgently? No trouble, I trust? Not expelled, I hope? We do have standards here at Wickham…'

And here the Headmaster's shaggy eyebrows rose anxiously, and Posie had to stifle a laugh. She coughed and made something up on the spot.

'No, of course not. We've just returned from India ahead of time. Little Harry's a good boy. I'm sure he'll fit right in here.'

That trip to India. Again. Posie was almost beginning to believe the story now herself. Heaven only knew why: she had absolutely no connection to India whatsoever.

Posie was amused though to watch Mr Doge nod with obvious relief and then she listened politely as he rattled on about class sizes, and school uniforms, and then, very delicately, he approached the question of school fees. He passed her a brochure tied with a ribbon and all the bits of paperwork he had fetched.

'So you'll consider Wickham Academy seriously then, Mrs Eden?' he asked nervously.

'Of course.' Posie nodded sagely. She poured the paperwork into her carpet bag without looking at it. She suddenly had the uncomfortable realisation that she was being dismissed. This wasn't what she had planned at all!

She had expected to be introduced to Dr Winter (or Mr Florizel, as he now was). What was going on? Wasn't Dr Winter here, after all? Had Constable Smallpenny made a horrible mistake? Or had Prudence, in booking the meeting, messed it up somehow?

'Frightfully sorry,' Posie began calmly, 'but I had wanted to meet your Master for English Literature. I had expected to meet him today. Your Masters normally don't leave until right before Christmas, do they? That was the reason little Harry wanted to come here, after all. In fact, we had a personal recommendation that the literature teaching here was excellent.'

More small white lies. Posie flaked off another bit of Watermelon nail varnish underneath the desk.

Mr Doge coloured. *Was it just possible that he was in on this with Dr Winter?* That he knew that in his English Literature Master he had none other than one of the top surgeons in the country? Was he shielding him?

'I'm really very sorry, Mrs Eden. I *had* expected you to meet Mr Florizel, as per your request. It's true, he is a truly excellent teacher. And he's a Housemaster, which means he stays here year-round, looking after those boys who don't or can't go home. He lives in the grounds. So that should normally be no problem.'

He coughed with some embarrassment and fingered the horrible paperweight on the desk nervously:

'I'm afraid that was why I kept you waiting so long. I've been trying to find Florizel myself, along with most of the boys in my care. I can't understand what's happened to him – he was supposed to join you on your tour of the school – I can only think he's been called away to some sort of emergency in his Schoolhouse. It's not like him to be flighty: he's utterly dedicated. I can only pass on his apologies and wish you a safe trip home.'

Thwarted, Posie could only smile sweetly and leave.

Mr Doge walked Posie down endless echoing corridors which still smelt of sweat and gravy and old plimsolls, and left her rather formally at the large Entrance Hall with its gold-inscribed boards showing those who had made it into Oxford and Cambridge on specific years. It also showed those old boys who had died in battle in the Great War. There were a good many names listed and the gilding looked very fresh.

Posie made a show of looking at her wristwatch.

'If you don't mind, Headmaster, I'll take a walk through your lovely grounds. My train is not for another forty minutes, and I have rather a "head" on me, which this sharp air might just clear.'

Mr Doge sniffed unhappily. Outside the rain was practically torrential. Wickham Academy was in a remote spot and although the grounds might have been described as beautiful on a sunny summer's day, they were just a blur of endless greys and browns today, even to the Headmaster, who loved the place dearly.

'As you like, Mrs Eden. But you are welcome to sit in our Library and wait it out. It may be more comfortable? At least, do you have an umbrella?'

Posie brandished her trusty black Brigg, which she had mercifully remembered, and set out as if she hadn't got a care in the world. Which was very far from the truth.

****

The boathouse on the River Wick was beyond the school playing fields.

Posie found herself there without meaning to, having walked through the wet grass and gravel paths in an absent-minded fashion.

For a few seconds along the way she had fancied that she was being followed; but after scanning the remote landscape and empty school premises she banished the thought from her mind, putting it down to a mere flight of fancy. Who was around anyway on such a horrible day apart from a few lonely schoolboys trying to kill time in their Christmas holidays?

The boathouse was an old Victorian building in dire need of a lick of paint. A single floor above was all closed up, presumably for storing the rowing boats in over winter, and underneath, in the murky water, a few small boats were lashed together, rocking in the current caused by the rain. The smell of damp rotting wood pervaded everything. The place felt horribly deserted and inhospitable. To make matters worse, the wind was getting up.

A long thin jetty jutted out beyond the boathouse over the water and Posie found herself unaccountably drawn to it, walking to the end of it. The wind came in big gusts off the river and she stood firm. She closed her Brigg umbrella for fear of being blown into the water and watched the wide span of the brown river beyond, rain-pelted and choppy. Frozen reeds and rushes blew about in a frenzy.

In every direction all you could see was the river and the marshes, and in the distance a wash of yet more empty wintery fields. Land and sky blurred together in a grey smudge and clouds the colour of lead scurried overhead. A brave family of moorhens swam by, the only other sign of life. Posie breathed in the salty-damp air, wishing she were safely back in London.

After a few moments of useless contemplation she resolved to herself to leave promptly and catch the next train up to Cambridge. She walked back along the jetty, not looking ahead of her, but checking her wristwatch for the time. A voice, unbidden, made her almost jump right out of her skin.

'You always did take risks, Parker. You looked like you were going to topple over there for a minute. I thought I might have to come in and save you.'

Blocking her path at the end of the jetty was a very tall and straight-backed figure wearing a black floor-length gown. His arms were crossed underneath it, as if for warmth. He wore no hat on his fair head and he had no umbrella.

Once she had recovered herself she gave a light laugh, much lighter than she really felt. For here he was. At last.

'And would you have saved me, Dr Winter? Or should I say, *Mr Florizel*?'

Dr Winter gave a humourless bark of a laugh.

'That's what I was trained for, wasn't it? To save lives. Training like that doesn't desert you that quickly.'

Posie drew closer. They were standing just a couple of feet away from each other now, staring at each other, the rain lashing down on both of them. The rain ran in rivulets down the back of Posie's felt cloche hat, running down her neck like unwelcome clammy fingers. She wanted the shelter of her umbrella, but the wind was too strong out here and Dr Winter didn't seem in a hurry to move. He was still blocking her path. Why didn't he let her pass?

Something in his keen gaze told Posie to beware. There was something about the way he was holding his arms under his gown, as if he was holding onto something delicate or dangerous. Her gut instinct kicked in and suddenly a random and completely unwelcome thought entered Posie's mind and she had to stop herself from gasping aloud:

He's going to shoot me.

Sure as bread is bread he has a gun under his gown.

She felt sick in the pit of her stomach and her pulse raced. She was trapped, with nowhere to run to. She was like a fly caught in amber, standing all alone at the edge of a river with nothing but her trusty gut instinct and a big umbrella to fight back with.

What a silly little fool she had been to think she could just arrive and have a cosy chat with Dr Winter, all pally-pally! What a little idiot Posie had been to imagine that Dr Winter would offer up all his hard-won secrets out of the very goodness of his heart.

And suddenly, too late, Posie remembered Professor Winter describing his altercation with his son years ago over Perdita; the hurt and bemusement which had lain behind Professor Winter's words:

'He threatened me with a gun once... Underneath that cool calm exterior of his I wondered just what sort of a son I had sired.'

So he was certainly capable of it.

Posie swallowed uncertainly, waiting for Dr Winter to draw his weapon. Time seemed to pass very slowly.

But nothing happened.

Her pulse slowed a little. She chided herself for her rash thinking and counted to ten in her head, trying to calm herself.

She was wrong! She was wrong! There was no gun. This man was a doctor, after all; as he said, he had been trained to *save* lives, not take them. For once the famous Posie

Parker gut instinct must have been decidedly off-kilter. Posie willed herself to keep staring at the man in front of her, undaunted, as if she trusted him completely and always had; as if they were simply two old colleagues catching up for old times' sake.

'How did you find me?' Dr Winter asked quietly, calmly, still not moving from his place on the jetty. 'I've spent more than four years here, lying low, wondering if I'd ever be discovered. I'd convinced myself I'd managed it. I'd got away with it.'

His voice was calm, unruffled. At last he indicated with a nod behind him to the scanty shelter of the boathouse and Posie followed him, thankful to get out of the rain at last. She noticed he walked with a pronounced limp, as the Porter at Trinity College had mentioned.

'That was your undoing,' she said in as normal a fashion as she could manage to his retreating back. 'You'd become complacent, sir. You shouldn't have gone to Cambridge on Monday, to that Memorial Service. You were seen. By your own wife! By Felicity. She thought she'd seen a ghost!'

Dr Winter rolled his eyes as if in disbelief.

'I hoped against hope that she hadn't seen me. I saw *her* of course, for the first time in five years. She looked like a professional widow. Like she was revelling in it.'

'She certainly still carries a candle for you, sir. She told me she'd never marry again. Owed it to your memory. I was quite surprised, sir.'

Posie heard Dr Winter make a harrumphing, dismissive noise from up ahead.

They reached the boathouse and stood there together awkwardly. Posie stole a sideways glance at him as he lit a Turkish cigarette with a match. So *that* was all he had been holding under his gown! Just a packet of ciggies! She breathed a sigh of genuine relief and noticed how his right hand shook almost uncontrollably as he steadied the flame.

She watched him from under her wet eyelashes, stealing glances at his profile. He was still handsome, but he looked older, much older than when she had last seen him in France. His likeness to his father was even more pronounced now. However, there was still something there which she didn't altogether like. He looked physically well and he was immaculate, clean shaven and well fed. But she couldn't rid herself of the feeling that his presence was like that of a snake in the boathouse; ready to pounce on her whenever it suited him.

'I *had* to go to that Memorial Service,' Dr Winter said shortly. 'I thought I wouldn't be noticed; I wore my gown so as to blend in with the other fusty old academics and I kept to the shadows at the back. I owed Neil Rolly almost everything I knew. The fact that he died of a heart attack and not out in the field of battle doesn't mean he wasn't a war hero in my book. Thank goodness he left our unit before that appalling bomb blast. He worked further up the line for the rest of the war, and then tirelessly these last four years repairing facial war wounds in London and in Cambridge. Pioneering stuff. They're calling it 'plastic surgery' now. I've followed his progress in *The Lancet*, which I buy from time to time. That man deserved recognition. I wanted to be there. Pay my respects.'

A silence followed in which Dr Winter smoked with relish and occasionally glanced over at Posie.

'You've changed, Parker,' he said, after a minute or so. He took a deep drag on his cigarette. 'During the war I wouldn't have given you a second glance. You've changed for the better, I mean.'

Posie almost choked in disbelief at the backhanded compliment but she swallowed her anger down.

'You've changed too, sir,' said Posie calmly, without adding the compliment on at the end.

He stubbed the cigarette out on the damp stone wall of the boathouse with a jabbing motion. He had obviously decided to stop with the niceties and cut to the chase. He watched Posie intently.

'*Why* exactly are you here?' he asked curtly. 'I smelt a rat the minute I was told someone wanted to meet me. I mean, why would someone come all the way out here into the sticks, out of term-time, to meet some bit-part literature teacher in a third-rate school for boys? So I watched you arrive and then I followed you on the tour you were given by that fat lad, Evans. I wasn't sure at first: you've cut your hair, and, as I said, you've changed. But I realised pretty quickly who you were. I got the shock of my life. Felicity send you here, did she? You mentioned her just now. To do her dirty work for her? Funny, I don't recall the two of you being pals in the unit. I don't remember her having *any* pals, in fact.'

Posie shook her head. 'I'm not her pal, and no, Felicity doesn't know I'm here. She doesn't even know that I've found you, or where you are. But I *am* working for her. She asked me to find out what had happened to you.'

Posie explained about the Grape Street Bureau, about her job as a Private Detective, about how she was here today posing as a parent. She watched Dr Winter for a reaction, but saw that his face remained smooth and impassive, giving nothing away.

'Shall we walk along the river and talk as we go?' said Dr Winter, in what was less of a question and more of an order. 'I need to get back to the school and it's on your way if you're heading to the train station.'

Posie nodded. She had no other choice really. She put the Brigg up over both of them. Dr Winter hardly seemed to feel the rain though. He dragged his leg markedly as they walked along the line of the river on a bloated muddy tow path, passing the sweep of the school fields on their right-hand side. The silence became unbearable and so Posie, now reassured of her own safety, started cautiously with her questions.

'So what did happen to you, sir?' Posie asked softly. 'People thought that you had died. Your parents thought you had died, too. You're listed as missing in action. You *should* have died. The Clearing Station took a direct hit, for goodness' sake!'

Dr Winter dug his hands down further into the gown.

'Of course I should have died. I do realise that, Parker. Practically every other poor blighter in that place did. But for some reason I was spared. One minute I was operating on a particularly difficult shoulder wound, and the next minute I woke up under some gorse bushes in the mud, lying in the undergrowth. I thought at first that I'd died, and that I was still there, in Arras, for some reason, just looking down on everything. Must have been the shock of the thing.'

He lit up another cigarette and inhaled. 'I must have been lifted clear somehow and dropped from several feet up in the air. I was fine. Well,' he indicated his jittery hand and his leg, 'as fine as *could* be, in the circumstances. Fine enough to get the very devil out of that place.'

'But what about Felicity?' asked Posie.

'What about her?' asked Dr Winter. He scowled. 'Terrible woman. *She* was the reason I ran off. As I was lying there under my gorse bush watching the carnage of the bombsite, who do I see come along and start wailing like a banshee but Felicity. She got down on her knees among all the debris and bodies and started blubbing. She got herself into a real state. Looked like some sort of vexed hedgehog snuffling about. It was terrible.'

Posie had stopped and was looking at Dr Winter incredulously.

'But that was understandable – she was your wife, sir! She thought you'd just died! What did you expect her to do? Sing a song of sixpence and start dancing the can-can?'

'Look here, Parker. I admit it; I'd made a mistake. I should never have married Felicity. She reminded me of someone from my past. It was my fault, I suppose. You know what they say; 'marry in haste and repent at leisure.' Well, I was certainly repenting by then, let me tell you.

And I decided on the spur of the moment that I wasn't going to spend the rest of my life repenting. No, thank you! Two months was enough!'

'Was Felicity really so bad, sir?'

'Worse. The marriage was a nightmare. Awful from the beginning. The gloss wore off very quickly. I was bored out of my brain. Every second of it was an agony. Just because she reminded me of this person from my past didn't mean she *was* her. In fact, they were polar opposites. Felicity was so cold, so unfeeling, and an arch catholic to boot, too: something she never mentioned in the first place; so she'd never have agreed to a divorce, more's the pity. All she could talk about was nursing, and being "efficient". She was a bag of nerves, too. Always asking me if I thought someone or other hated her. Verging on the paranoid, I'd say. Sometimes she read a fashion magazine, but that was the extent of her tastes in literature. She didn't have any creativity, either. I told her time and again about my love of the theatre and books but I swear to goodness she was never listening. Can you imagine? Being tied to such a creature for *life*? It was like being married to an ice-block. I think she was incapable of any love or passion. Wretched woman.'

Posie would have agreed with him once, but now she wasn't so sure: the fire in Felicity's eyes when she spoke of her husband and the photo she still carried in her wallet told a sort of love story. And Dr Winter was wrong: Felicity made hats, so she *was* creative, after all. Had these two ever really spoken to each other when they were courting? It seemed unlikely. It also seemed incredible that they could have married and remained at such cross purposes, but what did you expect when a marriage was based solely on looks, and the looks of a third party, come to that. But Posie kept quiet.

'So I took my chance and I got out. I ran from the marriage, I suppose. It just happened that I had to run away from my old life, too, in order to get away from Felicity. But it was a small price to pay for my freedom. And I'd never have worked as a surgeon again with *this*, anyway,' and he shook his right hand uselessly. 'I saw that instantly.'

'And your parents, sir? Wasn't it a bit hard on them?' Posie didn't mention that Dr Winter's mother was now dead; she didn't feel it was her place to impart such sad news.

'My parents are the kind of people who only wanted to know me if I was a big clever doctor, so I thought I'd cut loose from everything; let them all think I'd died. Well, in a way I had. Besides, my mother is one of those overbearing types, suffocating on an only child. She expected me to be in touch with her all the time, even from the front line. It was exhausting, so I cut loose from that too. So you see, my disappearing didn't matter much, anyway. I haven't been in touch with anyone since the war.'

Posie was intrigued.

'How did you manage it, sir? Felicity said you left all of your identity papers behind. How did you travel and work later on?'

'Oh, that was the easy part. There were hundreds of our boys, all injured, being loaded up on to frigates bound for England. There was no way they were checking any paperwork. Once I got to Folkestone I contacted some lads I'd helped to patch up a couple of years earlier; lads from the East End of London. That's the thing with being an army doctor – you meet all sorts. These boys were gangsters, but they had the biggest hearts. They were big-time criminals, permanently in and out of jail for counterfeiting and smuggling. They counterfeited my papers quickly; we invented Mr Florizel, who had an impeccable pre-war teaching career in a subject no-one would ever think me capable of teaching. This was the first job interview I walked into, and I've been here ever since. Happily, I might add.'

Posie suddenly noticed that they had gone rather a long

way along the tow path and were still trudging along by the river with no sign of turning right up towards the school buildings. In fact, they had gone so far along that they had left the comparative safety of the school way behind them. They were quite alone.

'I say, Dr Winter,' said Posie, frowning, coming to an abrupt stop. 'I need to get to the train station and we seem to have ambled along rather far. Or is this a short cut?'

Dr Winter jiggered around for another cigarette in his gown, ignoring her. He carried on talking as if she hadn't spoken at all.

'Funny, isn't it? How *names* can be misleading. I've often thought about it. Felicity means 'happiness', but I bet she never made anyone happy her whole life, certainly not me. And do you remember Helena Llewellyn? Poor old thing; named after a woman whose face launched a thousand ships, and yet *she* was plain as a farmer's wife. Great big turkey of a girl. I thought I'd try something different for once, and she seemed a good enough egg; made me laugh a good deal which was nice back in those hellish days. But I would have run away from her too. She wasn't my type at all; don't know what I was thinking about really. At least I was able to extract myself from that situation easily enough.'

'Because she died a horrible death, sir? Is that what you mean? How very convenient for you. And there we all were, thinking you were actually quite upset when you received that telegram!'

'Oh, I was. It was a shock. It was ghastly. But you know what? In a way I was relieved too.'

That this insufferable, selfish man could talk about girls in this horrible manner made Posie feel slightly sick. She was desperate to leave.

'Look, I have to go, sir. So *what* exactly do you want me to report to Felicity? I need to tell her something about what's happened to you.'

Out of the corner of her eye and behind Dr Winter she thought she saw a blurry group of people in the far distance coming towards them down the path. They looked as if they were dragging something heavy behind them, but Posie focussed instead on Dr Winter's face. He smiled slowly.

'Oh, *you* won't be reporting anything, Parker,' he said assuredly, breezily. 'Felicity's probably getting along very nicely without me on her War Widow's Pension. What more does she need?'

'She tasked me with finding the truth. That's my job.'

'And is your job worth risking your life for?'

'I'm sorry?'

'Why on earth do you think I've told you everything so far? It's certainly not so you can go simpering back to Felicity Fyne and offer up the details of my current life. Don't you understand? It's not my problem anymore. *She's* not my problem anymore.'

'She's your WIFE, sir! You've already told me yourself that there's no way you can get a divorce! So you're still well and truly married in the eyes of the law. So she *is* your problem still.'

Dr Winter's face had gone a strange mottled blue-grey colour, and he had pressed his lips into a thin line. When he spoke again it was in a low whisper and Posie had to strain to catch the words:

'How well you understand the situation, Parker. And now *you* too have become a problem for me. But unfortunately for you I can't run away anymore, so *you* are going to have to vanish this time. Into the river, forever. I can see you're the annoying sort of little madam who can't be trusted to keep her mouth shut, and I simply can't afford to pay you to keep quiet as well. So I see no other way…'

Too late Posie heard a tell-tale click and saw a small shiny black automatic pistol in Dr Winter's hand. He must have had it concealed the whole time up the sleeve of his gown.

She had been right all along.

The gut instinct had never let her down yet. Posie breathed through her mouth, willing herself not to panic.

Dr Winter trained the gun on her now, his right hand shaking profusely, and his left hand clutched over it for control.

'No one will find you. No one knows you're here, do they? No one will look for you either. Why, you should have left at least half an hour ago! And when your body falls into the river it will be washed along very quickly; the current here is very strong. It will most likely end up in some fenland boggy marsh. And months later, when it is found, no one will think to connect it with a low-life Private Detective who once made a nuisance of herself at Wickham Academy, pretending to be a would-be parent.'

Strangely enough Posie was very calm.

She had been in this situation before, of course, when she had been held hostage by a world-famous criminal who had toted a loaded gun about with far more panache than Dr Winter ever could. But it was the presence of the group of figures, a woman in a headscarf and two blonde little boys, coming closer, being blown about by the wind, who really gave her a sense of safety. Dr Winter hadn't seen them as he had his back to them. They were too far off to see what was really happening.

Dr Winter motioned Posie to move. Posie stepped back on the path, exactly where he wanted her to go, so that the river was right behind her; just one step away. But even among the fear and the madness, something Dr Winter had said rankled and stuck out as being strange. A bargaining chip.

'Did you just say you couldn't afford to pay me to keep quiet *'as well'*?'

Dr Winter didn't say anything. He just steadied his arm, which took a fair bit of doing.

'Someone else other than me knows your secret and has contacted you? Is that it?'

Posie gulped at the silence. She had nothing else to bargain with, so she'd try anything. Needs must.

'I didn't get around to telling you, did I? Felicity is being blackmailed, sir. The blackmailer seems to know all about you, and they're asking her for thirty pounds. They're threatening to contact the police, to try and take away her falsely-claimed War Widow's pension. But I'm guessing that *you* are being blackmailed too. Is that right?'

At his silence she kept talking.

'But *I* can help you, sir. I promise you. If you let me live I'll speak to the blackmailer this week, before Christmas. And I'll get them to leave you in peace. Forever. You'll never see or hear from me again, or from the blackmailer. And if you want, I can tell Felicity that you really are dead. For what it's worth I think she'll believe me.'

There was a whistling sound, a surprised intake of breath. But Dr Winter kept the gun trained on her.

'You're right. You sound as if you know who the black-mailer is, Parker. Do you? Someone who knows my whereabouts is very dangerous to me, for a number of reasons.'

'I *do* know who it is, sir.' She tried her best to sound convincing. She didn't need to admit to him that she had no cast-iron proof, just a series of hunches joined together.

The gun was lowered a fraction. 'Well? *Who*? Confounded scoundrel! Ruining my last two Christmases running and then sending me yet another request for money last week!'

Posie had been absolutely right. Dr Winter had taken the bait.

'I can't tell you who it is, sir. Not until everything is sorted. Did they ask you for thirty pounds too? And you paid it?'

Dr Winter nodded. 'Both times. It was all the money I had managed to save; virtually a third of my yearly salary. And you can imagine, we teachers earn a pittance since that wretched Geddes Axe programme of the government slashed our wages earlier this year.'

'Twice, sir? You paid thirty pounds, *twice*? Good grief! I promise I can help you, sir. Put this behind you. Now, please do put down the gun. We'll not get anywhere like this.'

At last Dr Winter lowered his gun and was looking at Posie with a modicum of interest mixed in with loathing.

'You're right,' he said, scowling, his gun slack at his side. 'This needs to be nipped in the bud. I just assumed the blackmailer was one of the East End lads who had made my new passport and teaching certificates; a kind of continuous payment. The cards always threaten contact with Felicity if I don't stump up the cash. Now *that's* a fate worse than death.'

'What were you going to do this time? Pay up?'

Dr Winter nodded. 'Yes. I'd have managed somehow. The last card made reference to criminal acts of mine being reported to the police. In addition to my cover being blown. Gracious, it doesn't bear thinking about!'

'What criminal acts would they be, sir? I don't follow.'

'BILLY? What *are* you up to?'

Dr Winter almost fell into the river himself in surprise as the woman who Posie had seen approaching on the tow path rapped him on the shoulder. The small group had now drawn level with them, and Posie saw that the woman was very, very pretty, with short blonde hair underneath her wet headscarf, somewhat uselessly set in a fashionable marcel wave, and tendrils of the hair were escaping in the wind and rain. The two boys were very small and looked almost identical to each other. They were clinging to the woman's tweed skirts. Posie saw at once that the boys were too small to be boarders.

'What on earth are you doing out here, darling? You'll catch your death! And who is this?'

The woman gave Posie a good long suspicious look. Posie and Dr Winter *had* been standing unaccountably close together and from a distance it could, she supposed, have looked a bit odd. The woman suddenly reminded Posie very much of Felicity Fyne. Who had, in turn, reminded Dr Winter of his first love.

A crazy thought came to Posie. *Had he found her at last?* Could this be the *real* Perdita? If so it would make for a peculiarly mad kind of logic, but it would mean that *something* had been achieved in all of this mess, which would be nice. She could stop hating Dr Winter quite so much if he had at least found his hearts' desire. All that searching had come to something.

Posie recovered herself. 'My son Harry is a prospective pupil here, and Mr Florizel was just showing me around the place.'

'Oh, I see.'

The woman turned to Dr Winter accusingly. 'All the way down here on this track, Billy? Bit far from the school, aren't you both?'

'Why, yes!' trilled Posie, smiling, feeling she owed some sort of explanation to smooth things over, still horribly aware of the gun close at hand.

'Mr Florizel was kindly humouring me. I wanted to get a full sense and measure of the place, you know. See if little Harry will like it. He adores nature, and rowing, too. So I absolutely *had* to see the river. I like to suss absolutely everything out first of all. And who are *you* exactly?'

The woman came forwards rather reluctantly, belatedly remembering her manners and extending a hand insincerely.

'I'm Mrs Florizel. William's wife. I'm very sorry but I'm not dressed up for company and neither are our sons. We didn't expect to see anyone around the place. We're just out collecting holly and ivy to decorate the living room of our Schoolhouse for Christmas. Except that we haven't found as much as I'd hoped.'

Posie turned to Dr Winter and gave him a barely-disguised icy stare full of disbelief.

Another wife!

She noticed that he had managed to hide his small automatic pistol again carefully. He had the good grace to look down at his black shoes in the mud of the path. Mrs Florizel turned to Dr Winter.

'I'm going to carry on looking for holly, Billy. Can you take the twins back up to the house? They're soaked through; all this rain! Get them in the bath. Hurry now! And then can you get the soup warmed up? The lads need to eat soon.'

And with that Mrs Florizel went on down the path, dragging a sack along behind her and casting quick nervy looks back over her shoulder.

Posie exhaled very slowly. She was almost certain that she was out of danger now, and the presence of the two little boys who were tugging at their father's gown almost sealed it. She could have kissed their wet little faces. When the boys started to run away from the river, up a stony path she had not noticed, Dr Winter and Posie started to follow them.

'Now you see the problem,' Dr Winter said softly, avoiding Posie's gaze.

'Is that *her*?' Posie asked blandly.

'Sorry?'

'*Perdita*. Your actress. I have to admit there's a neat symmetry to the whole thing. How did you find her?'

Dr Winter had narrowed his eyes and looked incredulous.

'How do you know about…? No, never mind, don't explain; I suppose you have your methods in your line of work. And, no. That isn't her, thank you very much. If you must know I *did* resume my search for the woman you speak of; her real name was Gloria Thummings. I couldn't forget her, obviously.'

He kicked at a stone on the path almost in anger. 'But when I got back from France I found Gloria had been dead at least fifteen years. I got concrete proof of it at last. Death certificates, the lot. The woman I had searched for since I was eighteen had been living in a damp flat in Glasgow, just around the corner from my parents' house, dying of rotting lungs for almost all of the time I had been searching for her. Gloria never worked as an actress again after *The Winter's Tale*, and she never read the newspapers, still less the theatrical notices. So she never knew I was looking for her. It was all so damned ironic. I could have helped her; saved her, probably. Even towards the end. It was all a total waste of time. A tragedy for her, though.'

Privately Posie wondered whether if Dr Winter *had* found Gloria Thummings with her rotting lungs he would have given her the time of day, let alone the benefits of his care and love. Gloria would have been much changed by her illness and Dr Winter was obviously a man who wanted physical perfection in a woman. Dr Winter was a fantasist, and not a particularly nice one at that. He had been living off a fantasy for years, and poor Gloria wouldn't have held up under the scrutiny.

Dr Winter glanced quickly up at his sons. They were running ahead over hard wet ground, throwing sticks and stones at each other as little boys like to do. Posie was sure that Dr Winter was a good father, but she was mindful of the gun which even now was lying concealed in the folds of his gown, and she was mindful too of how precariously her life had hung in the balance only ten minutes previously, and how it might still not be guaranteed. It was only a short walk to the school gates and then she would be properly safe and free of this monster; she just had to hold her tongue in the meantime and not rub the man up the wrong way.

'Who is this lady, then, sir?' *This lady who thinks she is your wife. More fool her.*

'I met Valerie, the twins' mother, when I came here. She was interviewing for the Matron's job at the school at the same time as I was interviewing as a teacher. She works as

149

the Matron here and we live here in the Schoolhouse with our two sons. It's all been most convenient.'

'Yes. I can see that.'

So, it was clear that Dr Winter was worried that his past would break through into his new life, for it was obvious that Valerie Florizel had no idea she was married to a man who didn't really exist and who, more importantly, was already married.

So Dulcie Deane had somehow found this out and was thinking of reporting Dr Winter to the authorities as a fraud and a bigamist. Both of which would carry a weighty jail sentence.

The school buildings came into sight and Posie breathed a huge sigh of real relief.

'So what will you do now, Parker?' asked Dr Winter, coming to a stop.

Get away from you and your gun, she thought quickly.

'I'll stop the blackmailer,' said Posie measuredly. 'As I promised. And I keep my promises. I'll send you a card to let you know when it's done, but I'll keep it as anodyne as possible, so your 'wife' Valerie doesn't think anything is amiss. I won't mention to anyone that I've seen you or know who you are. And I'll hush everything up where Felicity is concerned, too.'

'Tell her some sort of version of the truth, if you must, Parker. But not *where* I am. Got it?'

Posie nodded. 'And your side of the bargain is that you won't harm me, sir. You won't come looking for me with that gun of yours. Swear it? Please?'

Dr Winter nodded, his mouth a grim line. 'If I receive a postcard from you with news of a positive result by Christmas then you have my word I will never look for you again. Certainly. Otherwise, you leave me no choice. You've told me where you work, so don't think I won't find you. I have too much at stake.'

Posie gulped but nodded briskly. 'One last thing, sir.'

'What's that?'

'Get in touch with your father. He's a lonely old man and he misses you more than you know.'

'My *father*? What on earth has *he* got to do with all this?'

'I saw him yesterday.'

Posie was gratified to see Dr Winter turn even more ashen than usual beneath his normal pallor. Up ahead one of the boys had fallen down on the gravel and was screaming his head off. Dr Winter looked over anxiously in that direction.

'Really?'

'How else do you think I found you, sir? He told me about Perdita. The whole thing is almost unbelievable! That was the key to finding you, of course: your infatuation with a beautiful actress who had gone missing and your obsession with *The Winter's Tale*. I found you because of the copy of the play you kept in your tent: the inscription inside it. And it looks like leopards don't change their spots: you *still* choose women who look like that first actress. So now you have another Perdita, and, if you don't mind my saying so, sir, she seems to have you very firmly under her capable thumb, sir. You seem to be dancing to her tune. I hope you are happy, sir, happier than if you had stayed with Felicity. Let's hope for all your sakes, including your sons', that you didn't make a mistake when you "married" your current wife. I don't know how you'd run away from *this*. I wish you a good day, and a very Happy Christmas, sir.'

Posie turned on her heel before Dr Winter could reply and walked as fast as her feet would carry her in the direction of the big wrought-iron school gates. She looked back as she left and saw Dr Winter still standing there. Watching her.

I hope to goodness I never have the misfortune of meeting you ever again, she thought to herself numbly, almost running up the lane which led away from the school.

She felt slightly sick, and it wasn't anything to do with being hungry. Unusually.

* * * *

Twelve

Evangeline Greenwood was waiting outside the gates to King's College, a burst of bright red against the dark wet pavement. She was craning her neck up and down the street, checking for her visitor.

The college clock was just chiming a quarter-past two. Posie spied Evangeline from far off, and was grateful the woman had waited for her. She was late, which was a trait she detested in others, but after her horrible run-in with Dr Winter she had had to walk to the station as there were no cabs about, and she had missed her connecting train at Bishop's Stortford, having to wait for the next one.

On reaching Cambridge she had then discovered that there were no motor taxis at the station either and instead she had hailed a hansom cab and urged the driver to drive his horse as fast as he could into the centre of town. But it was an old nag, with no fondness for the wet slippery cobblestones, and even that short ride had seemed to Posie to stretch on forever. She had tried to push the experience with Dr Winter to the very far recesses of her mind, but she was still nervy and twitchier than she'd have liked to have been.

She dismounted with a tide of apologies and explanations, but Evangeline shook her head, smiling, and steered

Posie through the college gates and in the direction of the lovely old Chapel.

'Please, don't worry about it,' Evangeline soothed, walking smartly along. A crowd was gathered up ahead around the entrance to the Chapel. 'It is *I* who should be apologising after my awful behaviour on Tuesday. I do hope that you can forgive me. And thank you for coming. It was important to me.'

She turned her lovely purple eyes, so at odds with the exotic darkness of her long braided hair and dusky skin, on Posie, and it was as if the day had been transformed from a wet, wintry December day to a day in summertime with all the roses out and the birds singing. When she smiled it lit up her whole face and Posie saw for the first time that Simpkins the Porter had been right; Evangeline was a real beauty. Her bruise was either fading or covered very well with make-up, as it didn't seem so visible today. She was very dressed up, as if for evening, in a long golden velvet dress underneath the vivid red coat, and Posie noticed that large red rubies glittered at her ears, dancing with fire, even in the horrible darkness of the December day.

'What's this all about?' asked Posie, confused. 'I have to admit that I'm intrigued, but anxious too. Does it have a bearing on something to do with my brother, Richard? Did you know him? I don't even know that…'

Evangeline had stopped at the grand entrance to the Chapel and was purchasing a programme for each of them. She passed one to Posie with a smile but said nothing. Posie continued, slightly annoyed now:

'I showed you that letter which had been sent to me last year and you denied all knowledge of it on Tuesday, despite the fact that the letter specifically mentioned I should get in touch with the Secretary of Richard's Department, which turns out to be *you*. And who on earth is Harry Eden? I could swear you know something about all of this. Please, please, tell me. And what are we doing here anyway? This isn't Trinity College, where your husband and Richard were based. Why have you brought me here?'

They were suddenly inside the Chapel, and although it was only lunchtime, the interior was fully candle-lit. The glorious fan-like gothic glass interior of the walls and ceiling was lit up in a strange shadowy relief, both cosy and magnificent at the same time. The pews were filling up with bustling crowds now, tourists in raincoats and office workers taking a late lunch-hour. As Posie and Evangeline sat down on a bench very near the front, Posie finally read the programme clasped in her hands.

CHRISTMAS CAROL SERVICE

'But I don't understand,' hissed Posie, indicating the programme.

She was beginning to feel like she had been dragged out here on a wild goose chase, or even perhaps that Evangeline was not quite in her right mind; perhaps a bit dotty. Was that why the insufferable Dr Greenwood liked to keep her near him at all times? Posie noticed now that Evangeline had settled her red-gloved hands in her lap in a prim fashion and was checking her wristwatch and cocking her head a little to the back of the Chapel, as if waiting for someone else. A missing guest, perhaps?

She turned her lovely gaze on Posie again and half-sighed, half-smiled. She nodded quickly:

'You were right. It was *I* who sent you that note last year. I'd been thinking about trying to contact you for years. Since Richard died, in fact…'

'So you *did* know my brother, then?'

'Oh, yes. I knew him. I knew him very well, as it happens.'

Evangeline looked to the back of the Chapel again,

the way they had come in. There was much rustling of programmes and people were quieting down, expectantly.

Posie was willing Evangeline to continue, but she seemed to work to her own sweet rhythms, and wouldn't be rushed. Was this woman a former girlfriend of Richard's perhaps, or simply a work or research partner?

'I saw a story about you in the newspaper. That's how I knew how to contact you. I saw that you had become a Private Detective. I almost laughed aloud, as that was Richard's nickname for you, nosy parker! He would have been so proud of your success. He often spoke about you, and always with so much affection. I was so pleased you tracked me down, although I couldn't say so at the time. As it was, your visit cost me dear.'

She indicated her face. The bruise.

Posie gulped.

'Why did you deny you had sent that letter to me, then, on Tuesday?'

Evangeline exhaled slowly.

'Oh dearest Posie,' she said, avoiding Posie's gaze, 'when you are married to a first-class brute of a man like I am, you learn to lie about pretty much everything, as long as it makes your life easier. I couldn't admit that *I'd* sent the letter, could I? Even though it was obviously from me, and even though you had shown him the letter in all good faith the evening before. I had to brazen it out. It was more than my life was worth.'

She continued: 'I sent it to you last year, and when I got your reply I was mad with excitement. But my husband found your reply to me last year; he goes through nearly all my things and like a fool I hadn't burnt it. He went crazy, asking me what it was all about, but I played dumb, biding my time. I couldn't reply to you last year, and I was waiting for a good moment. It hadn't come yet. And then of course there was the *subject matter* of the letter. *That* was the biggest problem of all.'

'You mean whatever it was that my brother Richard supposedly left behind here?'

Evangeline nodded. Organ music started up. It was the first chords to 'Oh Little Town of Bethlehem'.

What was it Evangeline was talking about? Richard's research?

'I wanted to show you in person. In the flesh. I couldn't just write, or tell you. It's difficult…'

Posie suddenly remembered an expression used by the helpful porter, Simpkins. He had said, when talking about the Greenwoods, that '*it's all a bit tricky*'.

So he had been right.

Simpkins had led her to these people somehow, and now here she was. Sitting on a Friday afternoon, bemused, next to a woman she didn't know, about to listen to an entire Carol Concert which for some obscure reason still unbeknownst to her was important.

'I've been lying to my husband pretty much continually for more than eight years now, Posie. About what it was that Richard left behind.'

Posie stared at Evangeline stupidly. Was she talking in riddles?

A procession of choirboys in their smart red and white ruffed surplices suddenly processed past them, carrying candles and hymn-books and filling the huge high-ceilinged Chapel with unbearably sweet singing. They filed into their places in the choir stalls and finished the hymn.

Posie crossed her arms, and frowned. The opening bars of 'Once in Royal David's City' started up. Posie gave herself up to enjoy the music, trying to convince herself that her trip had been worthwhile.

And then she sat up stock-still in her seat, her back ramrod straight.

A schoolboy of about eight or nine had started to sing the first verse of the carol as a solo, and his voice carried out across the pews, clear as a bell and beautiful as an angel's.

But none of this was important, for when Posie looked into his face, she saw her brother's eyes, and her brother's lips moving to the old, old words. She was watching a miniature version of Richard, darker for sure, with pitch-black hair and a peachier-than- English complexion, but otherwise he was Richard; Richard as she remembered him when she was just a very little girl. Her heart was beating madly.

There was no miraculous piece of research after all; no breakthrough knowledge which Richard had discovered. It was even better. It was Richard's son. It had to be. The 'something' he had left behind.

So Posie had a nephew.

* * * *

His name was Harry. Harry Greenwood. Posie read it in the programme, which she scanned through as quickly as she could.

She had one thousand questions to ask Evangeline. But there was little time. Evangeline explained in a hushed whisper during the service that she was taking Harry for tea with his father at a smart hotel in town immediately afterwards. Dr Greenwood had been unable to attend the Carol Service, much to Evangeline's relief, and, luckily for Posie it had enabled her to see Harry in an open, legitimate environment, with no sneaking about or pretending. And it had been the perfect setting for Evangeline to show off her beautiful, talented son, with a voice which could move even the stoniest of hearts.

'You must be very proud of him,' Posie said sincerely as the two women walked out of the Chapel together after the service.

Evangeline nodded and smiled. 'Yes, I am. He's a good boy. He's talented and he has a good heart. Harry does very well at school in town, and he's a boarder there, which I'm pleased about it, as Harold treats him harshly at home. But I miss him when he's away. And I visit him whenever I can, which is every weekend, and for all his performances, like today. Now Richard is gone, Harry is my whole life.'

They stood on the wet paving slabs, some way away from the Chapel, waiting for Harry to come out of the vestry where he had been changing out of his robes. An icy chill wind was getting up, replacing the rain, blowing round the corners of the Chapel building.

Posie swallowed hard:

'Forgive me, but does your husband know that Harry is Richard's son?' There! She had said it.

Evangeline laughed, but it was a laugh without any joy in it.

'Yes, of course he does. How could he not? Harry is the spitting image of Richard, isn't he? It's an open secret. The whole college and the Department of Botany knows it, too, but no one, fortunately, has ever spoken of it. Especially not my husband, Harold. Who likes to admit to having been a cuckold? Better to save face and pretend. But he saves his anger up and it comes out in other ways.'

Posie nodded, remembering the bruise, and sadness flooded through her.

'I'm so sorry.'

'Oh, don't be. It's not just Harry. Everything I represent causes problems for my husband now. I came from a very wealthy family before I married him: my father was British but my mother was an Indian princess, and it was *she* who had the money, a great deal of money in the Raj. It was *she* who encouraged me to learn and to study; *she* who encouraged me to come to Cambridge and study botany here. I met my husband Harold here and fell in love. I didn't know he was a brute then, did I? Would you believe that he made me laugh? And he was so handsome. Still is, I suppose.'

Evangeline stared into the distance, but really Posie knew that she was staring into the past.

'My father agreed to our marriage and my Indian family settled a small income on Harold. But I was given a fortune, for myself and any children I might have. Thank goodness! It was put into a Trust Fund, so it's money which fortunately is now just for myself and for Harry. Harold can't touch it, which I suppose must be difficult. Living on the salary of a University Lecturer is hard and he doesn't like to ask me for financial handouts. So he punishes me in other ways.'

Posie nodded but she was speechless. All of this was so new, so daunting. *And she had a nephew!*

'And then there was my exoticism, I suppose. Harold loved it at first. It was a novelty. He was excited to walk beside a woman in the street who looked so different, so unusual, whom everyone stopped to look at. But it's been a blessing and a curse. The novelty soon wore off. He got tired of men staring, and of the attention I received. But I play up to it, to annoy him, I suppose. I always wear bright, bright colours. I have my clothes made in London in the most shocking, most jewel-like colours I can get hold of. I want to show him he can't daunt me, can't suppress me totally. Like he has done with my work.'

'Your work?'

Posie thought back to the way Evangeline had hidden away the blue folder when her husband had entered the office on Tuesday.

'Yes.' She nodded. 'I was a proper researcher at one point in my life. But after Harry was born, Harold forbade me to work. Some years later the position of Secretary in the Department came up, and I volunteered to do it for free. Harold let me; he thought he could keep an eye on me constantly, which is why he agreed to it; but I do it so I can continue my research. It's a smokescreen. I snatch moments here and there. Actually, it was *our* research to begin with; mine and your brother's. That's how I came to know him.'

She waved as a group of boys came out of the Chapel, loitering near the grand portico. Harry Greenwood was excitedly swopping what looked like cricket cards with some of the other choirboys, his surplice thrown carelessly over his arm in a ruffled knot which some poor devil would have to iron out later. Harry was tall, and the way he leant down now to the other boys, as if to take up less space and deflect attention from his height, made Posie gasp at the inheritance of her brother's self-same gesture.

'When I came to Cambridge I was working on plants used in medicines. I had studied that in Delhi, and I wanted to continue here. Of course, I knew I could never get a degree here, that women were not yet permitted to receive degrees in Cambridge, but I was thrilled to come anyway; to get the opportunity to study with other like-minded people. People like your brother Richard, who was interested in this same area. I became his unofficial assistant when he got his doctorate in 1913. I had been married a little over a year then to Harold.'

'Goodness,' said Posie, genuinely surprised at Harold Greenwood's recklessness at letting his lovely wife slip through his fingers – Richard Parker had been a very attractive man for sure, but much more importantly, he had had a brilliant sense of humour and an easy laugh –surely he would have posed some sort of threat?

'What did your husband think of you working with Richard?'

'Oh, not much at first. Harold was set on pursuing his career and climbing up the ladder as quickly as possible in college and in the Department, too. He had little time for me. But Richard had all the time in the world.'

She turned her purple gaze on Posie. 'So, you see what happened.'

Posie nodded. Suddenly everything made sense. She remembered her brother's strange unhappiness: the uncharacteristic moodiness; the way he seemed withdrawn, as if he had a problem he couldn't fix. And now she knew why. He had fallen in love. And Evangeline had been that worst sort of thing. Unavailable.

Posie was surprised, too, for her brother had usually been scrupulously moral in his actions, and getting involved with the married wife of a colleague seemed far off his usual behaviour.

As if she could read Posie's mind Evangeline laughed:

'I can see on your face that you disapprove. But don't! I'm not ashamed. These things are done. And I don't regret it for a minute. I'd do it all again in an instant; for Richard, and to have Harry. I'd give everything for both of them.'

Posie almost squirmed beneath the weight of the woman's honesty.

'My mother used to quote an old Indian proverb: *You never know where the heart will decide to rest*,' Evangeline said in a low voice.

'And it's true. We were in love, and it was inconvenient and dangerous. And it caused Richard much heartache. He asked Harold if he would agree to a divorce, but of course Harold said no. Harold thought it would ruin his career, that he would be a laughing-stock if I left him for Richard. We even said we would leave Cambridge altogether, go someplace else, so that Harold wouldn't be made to look a fool. But Harold still said no. Even when I told him about Harry; even when I told him that Harry was Richard's son. But he wouldn't let us go. In fact, it was worse than that; he threatened to get Richard arrested for trespass and adultery and a host of other trumped-up nonsenses. In the end it all came to nothing, but Harold threatened Richard's career here and made life very difficult for him in a number of ways.'

'So Richard knew that Harry was his son?'

'Oh, yes,' said Evangeline. 'Harry was born in 1914, and Richard tried to see him as much as possible. In snatched moments of course, like today. He was so proud of him. He was always talking about him. Harry was two years old in 1916 when Richard went off to war, and I made sure he had a photograph of Harry with him when he left. Harry used to call Richard "uncle", and it was fine, but I could tell that Richard minded. It was as if his heart were being ripped out, constantly. But he didn't know what to do for the best: we were at loggerheads with Harold and his career was about to be brought crashing down. I think that was why Richard volunteered for the war in the end. He felt he had to get away, rather than stay on here, hurting. Of course we didn't realise he would be killed. None of us knew the scale of the thing, the sheer uselessness of it all. What a waste! Even now, I can't believe it.'

Posie thought the same. Even now she couldn't believe it. And she also couldn't believe how little she had known her brother, either. How on earth had he shouldered the weight of such a big secret for so long without telling her?

'I have one quick question,' Posie asked in a hurry as the band of small boys had started to break up, hungry for their tea.

'Why did you sign that letter to me from Harry *Eden*? I don't get it?'

Evangeline sighed. '"Harold" was my husband's choice of name for "his" son. I shortened "Harold" to "Harry" which is more bearable. But when I was pregnant Richard and I nicknamed the baby "Eden". The baby was our little piece of paradise, that's why. The ultimate name for two botanists. I insisted that "Eden" be used as a middle name on the birth certificate for the baby; I lied and said that it was an old tradition in my family, that unless the name was used, the baby wouldn't be entitled to any of the Trust Fund in the future. Absolute balderdash of course, but Harold swallowed it. Hook, line and sinker.'

'And wasn't it awfully reckless of you to sign the letter in that way? Your husband works at the Department, after all. He saw my reply to your letter last year, after all…'

Evangeline shrugged, almost carelessly:

'Maybe it was reckless, but who cares? It felt good to be using the name we chose for our baby in public. It felt right to see it on the front of an envelope. It made it "real". Made it thrilling. Who knows what the future will bring? One day I hope to be able to explain to my son who his father *really* was. It goes beyond the bounds of reality to expect that Harry will adopt the surname "Parker", but who knows? Maybe he will ditch his current surname and use his middle name instead? Names aren't that important, really, are they? So many people ditch one name and take another; whether the name is real or made up, and whether they can lay claim to it or not. It will be up to him to decide. Anyway, I thought I should let you know about him.'

Harry was coming over, his face turned upwards, expectant with interest. Evangeline whispered so only Posie could hear her:

'I owe it to you and I owe it to Richard. I want Harry to have a connection with his real father. You might like to visit us sometimes, as his special "auntie"? But my husband mustn't find out, it's more than my life is worth. I can tell Harry that you've been living abroad, in a far-off land. And that you've just returned, if that suits you?'

Posie nodded, excitement filing her very core, the earlier events of the day paling into total insignificance; even the horrible Dr Winter with his wretched gun seemed a million miles away. Evangeline's description of her sounded eminently sensible. And somehow very right. Hadn't she been lying her head off recently about returning from a trip to India?

'Hullo, Harry!' She put out her hand to Harry and she had to stop herself from trembling as he shook it in a bemused manner and stared at her quizzically as only little boys can. For here was an outcome she had never imagined was possible. What a shame her father hadn't lived to know he had a grandson.

'I'm starving, mummy,' Harry said, turning his father's blue eyes up to Evangeline hopefully. 'Is this funny lady coming with us for cakes?'

* * * *

PART FOUR
Afternoon of Friday 22nd and Saturday 23rd December, 1922

Thirteen

Back at her desk at the Grape Street Bureau, Posie sat with her head in her hands, thinking. The day had been long, and surprising, and fruitful, too.

The luminous hands of her desk clock showed it was almost half-past five. The light had fallen a couple of hours ago, and the office was very quiet. Prudence had left early, Christmas holiday bound, and had expressed her thanks at the gift Posie had offered; promising to unwrap it on Christmas Day itself.

In return Posie had received a small box of Brazil nuts dipped in a cheap chocolate. She ripped off the foil covering carelessly and delved into the box. She ate a sweet slowly, crunching down noisily, and thoughts crowded into her mind.

Mainly she was thinking about secrets.

She thought about Dr Winter with his many secrets which he wanted to remain hidden, and she thought too about her new nephew, whose true identity was also a kind of secret.

Posie thought briefly of Felicity Fyne, sitting waiting for news in her hat shop in Hampstead. *What on earth was she going to say to her?* That Felicity wasn't a widow, or entitled to her War Widow's Pension? That it was a good job she didn't want to marry again as she wasn't legally free to do so? That her husband was alive and well, and that he was a bigamist with two sons and a pretty new 'wife'? And that he had forsaken his whole identity and way of life simply because Felicity was too awful a person to live with? Nobody deserved that sort of an explanation.

Besides, she couldn't contact Felicity yet: she still hadn't resolved the question of the blackmail which was part and parcel of the whole case. It was all very well if Dr Winter was willing to pay up, but there seemed no question that Felicity *could*, and the whole sorry mess needed to be sorted out once and for all.

Posie was troubled. There was a level of vitriol behind the blackmailer's threats which seemed malicious and personal, as if they wanted to cause intense hurt, or perhaps wreak revenge. So surely there was more to it than just money? But what motive would Dulcie Deane have for hurting Dr Winter and Felicity Fyne so badly? Why did she care so much about them? They had been a source of gossip in the past, for sure, but not much more so than anyone else. Had Dulcie harboured some strange love for Dr Winter which went beyond the normal schoolgirl crush which most of the nurses had felt for him at some point? If so, more fool her, thought Posie grimly. The man was a first-class horror.

But if Dulcie Deane had also somehow survived that bomb blast, and had returned to the life she had lived and loved before, even choosing to stay in the same hostel on Rupert Street, why on earth was she working like crazy at several jobs? Why did she need money so badly? Why wasn't she working in just *one* hospital for a decent salary like the trained, professional nurse she was?

Had something happened to her? Something didn't add up.

But who was Posie to know the secrets of Dulcie's life. So many people had secrets; so many people had different and borrowed identities.

Just then something tugged at Posie's brain; a forgotten phrase, a half-remembered memory. Then it went again. Posie chewed her lip thoughtfully, her mind still scrambling. She sighed and turned a note over in her hands.

It was from Alaric. One side of small blue Basildon Bond notepaper covered in his spiky, almost unreadable handwriting. It had been waiting for her on her otherwise clear desk. She read it over again:

Po,

Talk went well. Out of town now for 2 days, quick trip back to Boynton Hall to check on hives. I'm driving the Triumph motorcycle, giving it an airing. Bikram riding in the side-car.

See you Christmas Eve up at Rebburn Abbey. Looking forward to it!

Love,
Al

p.s. There's an early Christmas present for you in your strong-box. I thought you might like to bring it up to Rebburn with you.

She was surprised. Never one for big displays of affection, the note felt cosy, companionable. Alaric and Posie had been together as a couple now for more than a year, but they had not spent Christmas together before.

Rebburn Abbey was the big old country pile up in the north belonging to her old friend Rufus, Lord Cardigeon, and his lovely wife, Dolly. They had invited Posie up to them for Christmas after the fiasco of the year before, when Posie had been forced to spend the Christmas holidays all alone in her office with only a cat and dog for company, due to a central heating breakdown in her London block of flats, and an unfortunate mix-up with Alaric. Unusual circumstances, granted, but miserable too. Posie had complained bitterly about it afterwards to anyone who would listen, with the result of having had several invitations foisted upon her this Christmas.

And Christmas with Rufus and Dolly and their twin baby daughters would be wonderful, if a little chilly, as Rebburn Abbey was notoriously draughty, but nothing a good, thick jumper couldn't solve. And the icing on the cake was that Alaric had been invited too.

On the whole Posie was looking forward to Christmas, and to spending it with Alaric, but just lately she had been aware of feeling worried about the way things were going between them; as if the permanent twilight world of their relationship, which seemed to involve lots of absences caused by Alaric's travelling, might not be leading to anything more certain. He lived with her when he was in London, granted, but only like a lodger, and their relationship was such a secret that even Alaric and Posie seemed to have forgotten it really existed sometimes. But now, here, perhaps, was evidence to suggest it *was* going somewhere.

She was just going over to the strong-box which she kept in a cupboard when she heard keys jangling in the lock to the main office. She went out into the dark waiting room and saw Len silhouetted against the glass-stencilled front door, taking off his tweed homburg hat and shaking out his umbrella. Unexpectedly, her heart lurched a bit and her pulse quickened. Len bustled in.

'Wotcha doin' standin' out here in the dark, Po? I thought I saw your office light on from outside on the street,' he said cheerily, snapping on a desk light. 'I've got some last-minute bits and pieces to finish up here before Christmas. How was Cambridge? Prudence said you'd gone up there again.'

And Posie told him what had happened, including the bit about Dr Winter and the gun.

Len exhaled noisily.

'Coo-ee! What a day, eh? A dangerous one too.'

Posie nodded and sank down on the couch, suddenly exhausted and aware of the fatigue which had been creeping up on her since her return to London. Len perched on the arm of an armchair, and they lapsed into a companionable silence. Mr Minks skulked into the room, and chose, predictably perhaps, to jump onto Len's lap and purr there.

Posie and Len had been very careful to keep things professional at work since their almost-relationship had failed back in 1921. They painstakingly avoided each other's offices unless Prudence or a client was about. Even now they avoided talking about Alaric and Aggie, their respective partners. They maintained a false sort of jollity.

If truth were told there was probably still a modicum of feeling on both sides for the other, but it would never be spoken of, or acknowledged again. In fact, this was the very first time which either of them could remember in more than a year when they had sat together alone, unchaperoned. That thought hung perceptibly in the air between them.

Len reached into his briefcase. He took out a grease-proof-paper parcel of something dark and sticky and offered it to Posie. She shook her head and he started to chomp away.

'I was over on Rupert Street today,' he said, between bites.

'Oh?'

'I thought I'd take a look at that restaurant, the Florence; the one you were going on about.'

'I wasn't "going on" about it,' Posie retorted archly. 'I simply said I went there with the Inspector. And? What did you think?'

'Lovely,' said Len nodding. 'Booked a table for New Year's Eve. It'll make a change from fishcakes at Kettner's; Aggie'll love it. And while I was there I took a look along the road. Went to see where the nurses' hostel was; you know, scene of my former crimes and all that. They've put up a brand new hostel in its place next door.'

Posie nodded. 'I was there too, yesterday. Nice new building, isn't it? I don't think you got around to telling me the original had been bombed. Is that how you lost touch with your girlfriend, then? The "stunner"?'

She saw Len colour, even in the dim light of the desk lamp.

He nodded and looked sheepish.

'Yes, it is, actually. I tried to locate her when I came back after the war, but with no success. The records had all been lost in the bombing; it was a total wipe-out. The only thing I could find out for certain was that my former girlfriend, Dora, wasn't one of those killed. Which was a relief.'

There's something else he's not telling me, Posie thought to herself. Len was looking slightly shifty. Thank goodness she hadn't taken up with him, she reminded herself wearily. She would have run herself ragged trying to keep Len's interest. And failed miserably, too. She even felt a bit sorry for Aggie, Len's annoying wife. Then she realised what Len must have done.

'Did you go in, today? To the hostel? Have a look around?'

Len nodded, his colour high. 'They've done it up nicely. That new style. It will look a treat when it's all finished.'

'And so you asked them, did you, if they knew Dora? If she'd come back after the bombing and was living there now?'

My gosh! Sure as bread was bread she had got it in one! Len's face was almost purple. He tried to shrug carelessly:

'Purely out of interest, of course. For old times' sake. But I got nowhere. They'd never heard of Dora, and she's not living there now. They don't have any details for her from before, either, as everything went up in the blast. Useless asking anyway, as the wardens are new. They don't know anyone from before the war.'

'*What* did you just say?'

'That the wardens are brand new to the place, although they seem to like pretending they've been there since the dawn of time. They didn't know me from Adam. I told you already, the previous one, like a watch-dog she was, was killed in the bombing, not that I was on the best of terms with *her*. But at least she knew me. These new ones are from Wales. Nice enough, but dismally slow. Why, do you know, when I got there I had to wait a good five minutes while they had a whole conversation in Welsh with one of their nurses! Can you believe it?'

But Posie's mind was racing and her heart was thudding, throwing itself against her rib-cage. For no apparent reason the words of Evangeline Greenwood earlier in the day came flooding back into Posie's mind, word for word:

'So many people ditch one name and take another; whether the name is real or made up, and whether they can lay claim to it or not.'

Everything came together suddenly, the puzzle pieces fitting tightly. Posie stared at Len with unseeing eyes. The smell of what he was eating suddenly seemed to overwhelm her, to take over the room. It was the same smell as yesterday, in the warden's office in the hostel. Sticky, sweet.

'Quick! Is that a ginger cake?'

Len nodded, bemused. 'I say, Po. Are you okay?'

'What did she look like, the nurse who was speaking in Welsh?'

'No idea really. I only saw the back of her head. But she makes fantastic cake! She was leaving a great big ginger cake with the wardens, and when I started chatting to the woman warden afterwards she insisted on giving me a piece, too. It was delicious. You missed a trick there, Po.'

Posie nodded bitterly. 'Yes. Yes, I certainly did.'

And then she got up and headed to the telephone to place a call.

'New Scotland Yard, please,' she asked the Operator. 'Fast as you can.'

* * * *

Fourteen

Things made more sense now. But it took a huge leap of the imagination to get to the solution she had just come up with. Posie felt that she just had to run the whole thing past Inspector Lovelace, even though it was now past six-thirty on the Friday before Christmas. And even though Felicity Fyne had expressly forbidden her from involving the police.

She held the telephone receiver anxiously to her ear and thought it all out. Someone was looking for Inspector Lovelace and she could hear muffled shouting on the other end of the line.

Posie had always assumed that the wardens at the hostel had been the *original* ones, and that they would have known the original Dulcie Deane from before the war, thus giving the current Dulcie Deane her legitimacy. But if they were newly installed after the war, along with the new hostel, why would they think to question a nurse who arrived and claimed she was Dulcie Deane, a resident of the hostel before the war?

Particularly if, like them, the nurse in question was Welsh, and friendly. Apparently she treated the wardens well, and baked them ginger cake, too.

It had to be Helena Llewellyn. Masquerading as Dulcie Deane.

But why? And could it be? Helena was supposed to be dead, after all. But if there was one thing this case had taught Posie, it was to keep an open mind. Especially when it came to those who were supposed to be dead.

'We're looking for the Chief Inspector for you, Miss Parker,' came a harassed-sounding voice the other end of the line. 'I'm afraid we can't find him just yet. Can you hold?'

'Of course.'

Posie was thinking nineteen to the dozen.

Yes, she told herself. *Yes, it could be.*

If Dr Winter had survived a direct bombing, then didn't it follow that somehow Helena Llewellyn could have survived a shipwreck? It seemed there was no end to the number of people who had, against the odds, survived the Great War and were now living incognito, in other people's lives, in other people's identities.

If the blackmailer *was* indeed Helena Llewellyn then the vitriol and revenge behind the whole campaign was completely understandable, and Helena would, if she were that way inclined, want to cause pain to both her former fiancée and his wife, the insufferable Felicity, the woman who had supplanted her in his affections.

But the Helena Llewellyn who Posie remembered was not like that. She was kind and forgiving, and she had had a good heart. So how could it be?

And another thing; why on earth was Helena not just living out her life as herself? It would be much easier. She had her own nursing qualifications and could presumably get a senior job for herself in a hospital in town somewhere. Why on earth was she pretending to be Dulcie Deane and living such a scratch existence?

A familiar voice came on the line. A distinctly unwelcome one.

'Parker? What is it *you* want? Make it snappy.'

It was Inspector Oats, an old adversary of Posie's. He

was an old-fashioned bobby-on-the-beat style policeman who did things the only way; *his* way. It would be fair to say that he hated Posie's guts, and thought her a timewaster and a busy-body, and she, in turn, thought him a bad policeman, not to mention an old stick-in-the-mud.

'Where's Inspector Lovelace?'

She heard his puffy intake of breath. 'I don't see as it's any of your business, little lady. But, as it happens, there's been an *incident*: his little daughter Phyllis has been taken bad with an 'orrid bout of pneumonia, an' they've got her in the kiddies 'ospital in Great Ormond Street.'

'Oh, gracious me,' said Posie, filled with concern. 'Poor Inspector Lovelace, and poor baby Phyllis, too. Is it serious?'

'Dunno. Is this a social call then, Parker? Can I 'ang up? Or were you after some genuine police input on summit?'

Posie caught the note of interest in his voice. The fact that he was giving her *any* time at all on the telephone struck her as strange. Posie needed urgent help, and if this was the only way, then so be it. It would be harsh on Helena, but it looked like involving the police was the only way. *Any port in a storm*, she told herself.

She forced herself to be polite, and reverential, qualities Inspector Oats seemed to prize above all others, including talent.

'Do you have time, sir? It *is* the Friday before Christmas after all…'

'Aye.' She could imagine the Inspector nodding his big head, getting his pencil and leather-clad notebook out, expectantly.

'As it happens I'm on duty here alone for the next two days. I'm on pre-Christmas cover and the place is fairly quiet. And you're in luck, I don't have many other cases on.'

What he means is he's bored silly! thought Posie with amusement. Inspector Oats was well known for being like a terrier, chomping at the bit for work, which, when it arrived, he would chase to the bitter end. He hated sitting around doing nothing, twiddling his thumbs.

'It's small fry, sir. A blackmailer, sir, but I want them stopped. In addition I think it may be a case whereby the person can be prosecuted for fraud, as well as false representation. Oh, and having fake identity papers too, and previous extortion offences. The person may also be claiming state benefits not rightly theirs.'

She knew that in mentioning the wrongly-claimed benefits she had ignited his interest: Inspector Oats had a pedantic bee in his bonnet about scroungers.

'Not such small fry then,' he harrumphed, sounding pleased. 'A first-class scrounger! Righty-ho. And mebbe we can get 'er with crimes of extortion under the Larceny Act if she's a blackmailer to boot. Can you give me the details of the case so far?'

Posie gave a quick outline without giving away the identities of either Dr Winter or Felicity Fyne, and she took care to omit the fact of Dr Winter's bigamy, a real crime which, sure as bread was bread, she knew Inspector Oats would pursue in the courts. She stated what it was that she wanted done next:

'Above all, sir, I think we need a warrant. I don't think that Helena Llewellyn will magically appear if I request a meeting, and she's got those Welsh wardens at the hostel eating out of her hand, so they'll protect her, come what may. Can you get one of your lads to seize her tonight when she returns to the hostel from work? Send one of your Constables over? Get her into an interview room?'

'Yep,' said Inspector Oats briskly. 'I'll do more than that, though, I'll get over there meself. No matter if it's a long wait. I'll call you when we've got 'er in custody.'

Posie agreed to wait on at the Grape Street office where the telephone was located and gave the Inspector the relevant details and the address of the hostel on Rupert Street.

'One thing, though, Parker. Are you going to be able to bring the victims of the extortion in, to press charges? Otherwise, who exactly is alleging a crime? I don't want this turning into a mare's nest, Parker. I do have targets to consider.'

'Mnnn, I'm sure it won't be a problem, sir,' said Posie breezily, knowing full well it would be downright impossible to bring either Felicity or Dr Winter in.

'But, regardless, sir, you can press charges anyway, on behalf of the Crown, can't you? If there are enough charges against the state, I mean, which there might well be. I just ask that I can speak to the woman before you formally press charges.'

'Mnnn, fine. You'll hear from me later.'

'Thank you, Inspector. I appreciate your help. Truly.'

'Bah, I'm just doing my job, Parker.'

And as he rang off, Posie tried to ignore the horrible feeling which came to her immediately that maybe she had got this all wrong; that Dulcie Deane was just Dulcie Deane after all, and that what she had just involved the police in was indeed a mare's nest of the highest order.

****

Len had left for the night, leaving a scrawled note wishing Posie a very Merry Christmas. Mr Minks was sulking in the kitchen, and wasn't in a cuddly mood at all.

Posie stood at the main bay window of the waiting room and looked down at the dark and empty street below, three floors down, at the lights of a café on Shaftesbury Avenue which twinkled through the darkness and the incessant freezing rain.

Posie felt unaccountably sad.

She felt bad about having got the police involved in arresting Helena Llewellyn, *if* it was Helena Llewellyn, and the more she thought about the woman, the more she felt sorry for her. She pictured her now, tired and aching after a long day's work, pleased to return to her single room at the hostel, looking forward to a bath and a book, perhaps. Except that tonight Helena would be met by Inspector Oats, which was no laughing matter. Then she would spend a night in the cold dank cells at New Scotland Yard.

If Posie had been right in her reasoning.

She felt quite alone suddenly, a feeling which fortunately didn't come upon her very often, as it brought its own depressing train of thoughts. *All these lonely women I've met*, she thought sadly: Felicity Fyne, without a husband, but sworn to him for life; Evangeline Greenwood, with a husband she detested; and now Helena Llewellyn, living life as someone else, with only a vendetta of revenge left to warm the cockles of her heart.

The telephone rang. Posie checked her wristwatch. It was only half an hour since she had spoken to Inspector Oats; it simply wasn't possible that he could ring back so quickly. The Operator put a call through from Oxford.

It was Alaric. He never messed around with niceties on the telephone.

'Well?'

'"Well," what?' Posie almost snapped down the line at him.

'Did you like it? What do you think? Too over the top?'

Too late she remembered his note and the present in the strong-box.

'Rats! I totally forgot. I haven't had time to open your gift just yet. Shall I get it now?'

'Never mind. Got to go. I'm at Oxford Station in their ticket office using the telephone and my train's just come in. The motorcycle conked out near Jericho and I've had to leave it with a garage here over Christmas, worse luck. But I'll see you up at Rebburn.'

He rang off. No love, no kisses, no anything special. Posie scowled and replaced the receiver into its cradle. She banged her way through into her own office. Alaric was insufferable sometimes!

She went to the cupboard where the strong-box was stored and took the key from a piece of string round her neck.

A small brown cardboard box was within, nestled among the petty cash. Posie sat down at her desk and opened the box. Inside was another one, this one made of black and gold-tooled leather. It was utterly sumptuous. On its outside it said:

CARTIER

Posie tried not to get too excited and took miniscule, teeny-tiny little breaths. She opened the box and closed her eyes.

There was a stunning rose-gold ring inside which caught even the dim light in the room and sparkled. A pale pinky-peach stone the size of a penny was surrounded by diamonds in the shape of petals. The whole impression was of a cheerful, sparkling daisy.

She breathed out slowly. A tiny note had been folded into the box too. She read it quickly:

Po,

I got this stone for you when I was in India. It's a pink sapphire, which seemed apt as you always see the rosy side of life. That's what I love about you.

I do love you, you know. Let's make it official for goodness' sake.

Can't think what took us so long.

Love,

Al

Posie slipped the ring on to her left hand ring-finger and grinned. Now she really did have a proper connection with India.

Just then the telephone rang again. The Operator announced a call from New Scotland Yard.

'We had a lucky break,' said Inspector Oats in bluff gratified tones. 'We got 'er just after we arrived. Want to come along now or wait until tomorrow?'

'Now,' said Posie, already grabbing at her carpet bag, her own joy and surprise at Alaric's gesture completely forgotten for the moment.

'I'm on my way.'

* * * *

Fifteen

'Any news on Inspector Lovelace's baby?' asked Posie on her arrival at Scotland Yard.

Inspector Oats shook his head dourly and led her down to the interview rooms.

'Your wee lassie didn't make a fuss at all, your lady blackmailer. She's not making one now, either. She's a rum one an' all. Just sits there, silently, like she's lost in her own world. You sure she's quite the ticket? I'll give you half an hour, Parker, and two of my Constables will be watching you through the two-way mirror, so no funny business. I expect you to help me, too. Afterwards. Give me a detailed list of the crimes I can charge her with. You know, you scratch my back and I'll scratch yours…'

The thought of this was too repulsive to even contemplate, for Inspector Oats bore an unfortunate and more than passing resemblance to a trout, but Posie smiled and thanked him anyway.

She was steeling herself for a confrontation with a woman she hadn't seen for years, a woman who had changed, who wasn't expecting to see her, who might not even recognise her…And was the Inspector right? Had Helena simply lost her mind? Could that be the explanation behind all of this?

Posie opened the door to the interview room which the Inspector had indicated and walked in briskly. She looked quickly at the person sitting at the single bare desk underneath the one bright lightbulb. Posie had to stop herself from gasping aloud, and recoiling in shock and disbelief.

The woman who sat there stared at Posie with familiar, huge, dark doe-eyes. She was very, very thin, almost emaciated, and about as far away as it was possible to get from being the large, buxom woman Posie remembered from the days in Arras. She was virtually unrecognisable.

The woman had short bobbed dyed red hair and was wearing a blue and white nursing overall. Posie thought that she looked as if she had saved up all the sadness in the world and kept it just for herself. But it was undeniably her.

It was Helena Llewellyn.

'Posie Parker?' The voice was the same, and incredulous. On the ball. Gone went the idea of Helena being mad, or incapable. Posie took the chair opposite Helena's.

'Good evening, Helena, or should I say, "Dulcie"?'

'Why are *you* here, of all people? You working for the police or something?'

Posie shook her head. 'I'm here in a personal capacity. But there are criminal charges listed against you, you know.'

Helena sighed and looked down at her hands. They were scabbed and calloused, the result of huge amounts of rough work. Posie's heart lurched when she saw that on Helena's ring finger she was still wearing the poor little pearl ring which Dr Winter had managed to buy for her in Arras. Posie found herself hiding her own hands in embarrassment, what with their well-tended skin and nails, and her very recent new and expensive pink ring from Alaric.

'What's this all about, Posie? For old times' sake, let's forget this and treat it as a misunderstanding, can't we? It's nearly Christmas, after all.'

Posie looked at the salmon-coloured charge-sheet on the table between them. She shook her head.

'There's quite a number of charges listed here, Helena. And if you don't help me out tonight, you'll hear them all formally read out to you tomorrow, with or without a solicitor at your side. That's your choice. So I don't think we can pretend it's all just a misunderstanding. Besides, *I'm* only interested in the charge of blackmail, of extortion. And you were happy enough to continue with that, weren't you?'

Posie was thinking how strange it was to be in this position, sitting here. She thought too about all the patients who had appreciated Helena in the past; all the kindnesses Helena had shown them. She remembered the real sadness when their unit at the Clearing Station had received the news that Helena had died. Ironically most of those who had mourned her had themselves now been killed, one way or another.

What had happened to the woman? Helena stayed silent, her hands in her lap. Posie changed tack:

'I *knew* you, Helena. I know you're not a bad person. You're a kind person. What's going on? I'm here because of Dr Winter and Felicity Fyne, and your threats to ruin their lives. I need you to promise me that it's going to stop. Then you'll walk out of here. A free woman. You have my word. Otherwise, I'll get the police to charge you formally tomorrow.'

For a moment Helena stared at Posie in a challenging way, and then looked to her side, away to the horrible olive-green painted wall. She was obviously considering what was the best course of action.

'Why did you have to bring me in here?' Helena said at last, a note of pleading in her voice. 'Why are the police involved? Couldn't we have had a nice chat back at my hostel?'

Posie laughed ironically. 'Come on, Helena. There was no way you would have met me for a chat, nice or other-wise, if you knew what it was I wanted to chat about. So what do you say?'

'Very well, then.' She nodded at last. 'What do you want to know?'

'Why are you pretending to be Dulcie Deane? She died in a bomb blast in Arras in 1918. You know that, don't you?'

Helena sighed:

'Of course I know that. But *I* supposedly died on a ship, the *SS Victoria*, which went down on Christmas Eve, 1917. I was on the list of passengers. But I didn't make the boat; my train to Dover was running ten minutes late and I missed the boat, fortunately or unfortunately, however you look at it. When I found out what had happened out at sea I turned heel and went back to my ma, in Wales, to let her know I was still alive. When I got back home I found chaos; my mother had been informed by telegram that I was dead, but worse, she had received a second telegram from William Winter, my fiancée.'

'Telling you the engagement was off?'

Helena nodded grimly. 'So you all knew he dumped me by telegram?'

Posie nodded. 'We all hated him for it, too.'

Helena continued. 'That evening was the end of my life as I knew it. My mother had had a stroke shortly before I arrived, and was left totally paralysed and without her faculties. She didn't recognise me, her only child. Imagine!'

'So what happened?'

'I was all my mother had in the world. We had no relations, and she had very few friends who would actually come and help. The prognosis wasn't good, and the doctors said she had little time left. So I decided to move her to a nursing home, a good one, and I sold everything we had to pay for her care. We didn't have much money, but I couldn't have nursed her alone; she needed several of us at once. Just before we moved from her house, my mother received a letter from the War Office. I opened it, naturally, and I read that due to my death on the *SS Victoria*, the War Office had decided to pay my mother a monthly pension as recompense. The first month's cheque was included. It was a godsend.'

Helena looked at Posie slightly defiantly. 'That monthly cheque kept us both going for the next few months. The care was ridiculously expensive, and I couldn't work as I was with my mother all the time. I had no place of my own, so I used to sleep on the floor next to my mother's bed, and they let me stay there, out of pity, I think. I didn't have enough to spend on food, either, which is when I began to lose weight. And once a month I'd collect this cheque at the Post Office. We came to rely on it.'

Posie was beginning to see the difficulty.

'I'd heard about the bombing of the Clearing Station at Arras, and I had read William's obituary in the newspaper in February 1918. I was sorry about his death. Despite what he had done to me, I wouldn't have wished that upon him for the world.'

Helena twisted the tarnished pearl engagement ring in what looked like a familiar habit. 'My mother died in the June, six months after her stroke. About the same time my mother died I also read a short article in *The Lady*, complete with photographs. It was about a beautiful blonde woman called Felicity Fyne, detailing the bravery of her husband, a war-doctor. A man she'd married on Boxing Day 1917 in Arras. A man who had died in February that year. A man called William Winter. And that's when I realised that rather than dumping me because I just wasn't the right person for him, he had rejected me in favour of this woman, this Felicity Fyne. I saw red.'

'I can imagine.' Posie nodded sympathetically.

'I had to do something. I didn't want to stay in Wales forever, not with my mother dead and buried, so I decided to move to England. The problem was, I had come to rely on this cheque every month. So I decided to continue drawing it, to not tell the War Office that my mother had died, and to not bother informing them that I was actually alive. I changed identities instead and became Dulcie Deane, whom I had known fairly well, and I was certain was dead. I remembered that she had had some connections in London, including a place at a good hostel, and being an only child like me, and a bit of a loner, there would be no family or real friends to make complications. But just in case, I cut my hair and dyed it red like hers; I'd already lost a lot of weight and I started to wear different clothes, as similar to Dulcie's as I could manage. I changed my writing, too, although I never had to write or sign much which could be compared to her real writing. It all went swimmingly, and I *did* manage to get a room in her name in the new hostel which was being built to replace the one she had actually lived in before the war. I was surprised at how easy it all was. I was extraordinarily lucky in that no-one was around from before the war. No-one remembered the real Dulcie, and no-one asked any tricky questions.'

'So what went wrong?'

'Two things,' sighed Helena. 'The first was that I had totally underestimated the difficulty in getting a job after the war. Nurses were ten a penny, especially as the world and his wife had been volunteer nurses on the front line, so London was saturated with all kinds of people who could claim to nurse. In addition, I didn't have the real paperwork as Dulcie Deane, so no proper London hospital would have me. I couldn't risk showing the paperwork I had as Helena Llewellyn, in case it was referenced back to the War Office and they realised I was drawing a cheque I had no claim to.'

'Was the cheque so important?'

'It's all that's kept me going these last years,' said Helena simply. 'It pays my board and food, which isn't much. Nurses get paid a pittance right now, or hadn't you heard that the government has slashed our wages? The jobs I take anyway are bit-part and they pay next to nothing.'

'I see. And the second thing which went wrong for you?'

'Once, in that autumn of 1918 I went for an interview as a Matron at a private school for boys, out Cambridge way. I didn't get the job because I didn't even go in for the interview. But while I was there in the waiting room I got the shock of my life.'

'Dr Winter?'

Helena nodded.

'There he was, alive and well, and interviewing for a job as a Schoolmaster, of all things! Calling himself something different, mind. But then I was doing the same thing, too, so I wasn't about to blow his cover. He didn't recognise me. In fact he just didn't see me. He looked right through me. He was flirting with some blonde piece of fancy who was interviewing for the same job as me. But crucially, it wasn't Felicity Fyne. I could see that much.'

'And?'

'I left the school in a state of shock. And then, afterwards, it overwhelmed me. The fact that he was alive and well and had ruined *my* life and perhaps caused my mother's stroke, too, was intolerable to me. It burnt me up. It consumed me. It became all I thought about. And I thought about Felicity Fyne too; her with her smug self-satisfied article in a glossy magazine, and her actions which must have stolen William away from me. I was jealous of her. There! I'll admit it! Jealous of a woman who didn't even know that her own husband was still alive! It haunted my every waking thought. My life was ruined, and I decided I would upset them both, too.'

'Ah,' said Posie. 'You started blackmailing them, you mean?'

'I never thought of it like that. And anyway, why should they get away with what they had done and live happily ever after? I hated them both. So I contacted them anonymously; told them what I knew. I thought I'd make a little money out of it, too.'

'That's blackmail, Helena.'

Helena shrugged. 'Perhaps. I suppose you *could* construe it like that, if you wanted to.'

'And Dr Winter paid up? But Felicity didn't?'

'That's right. Even though I knew she could afford to pay, so I didn't feel too badly about asking her for money. You should have seen the size of her engagement ring which she was flaunting around in all the photographs in *The Lady* article. Like an egg it was! And I desperately need money *now*. Work has practically dried up, so I thought I'd force their hands this year. I set Christmas Eve as the date for them to decide whether they would pay me or not. But how come you know so much?'

'I spoke to both of them, Helena. Separately. I am sorry for you, of course I am. The whole thing is tragic. But we need to fix this. You can't carry on like this; it's no way to live. What a waste of your life. You need to make your life count. You didn't *not* die on that boat for a reason, you know.'

A look of pleading entered Helena's eyes. 'What do I do then?'

'First, you need to promise me you'll stop hassling Dr Winter and Felicity. I understand they are both detestable to you, and in the case of Dr Winter I agree wholeheartedly with you, but I think they've suffered enough in their own ways without any more input from you, if that's any consolation. And you can't take these cheques from the government anymore; it's not right.'

Posie nodded, certain of what must be done now.

'With your agreement *I* will write to the War Office anonymously tomorrow and say your mother has now died and doesn't need the money anymore. Hopefully they won't ask for exact details about the date of her death. And then – and this is the hard part – *you* need to live; to become yourself again. Stop being Dulcie Deane, who is dead, and become Helena again; the Helena who was loved by so many people. You were adored. I know for a fact that even Felicity Fyne, who you never met, realised how much the men loved you. She was jealous of that.'

Helena started to cry. Silent tears ran down her thin tired face.

Posie continued. 'Why don't you move away from London? Move to a small town, to a backwater, or to another big city – take your pick – but get away from here. Start interviewing for jobs with your real paperwork, and stop scratching a living like you have been here these last few years.'

Helena nodded silently. She pointed to the pink charge-sheet:

'But what about these?'

'Leave it to me,' Posie said briskly, rising from her chair. 'You should be free to go again shortly. I wish you all the best in your life.'

'You too, Posie. You always were a brick. But I still don't know how you got involved in all of this?'

Posie rolled her eyes heavenwards.

'Felicity Fyne employed me, if you must know. I'm a Private Detective. She had got the shock of her life. She saw Dr Winter out in public, when she'd convinced herself he was dead, despite your best efforts. She thought she'd seen a ghost.'

Helena laughed, but it was a hollow sound.

'How appropriate. Since the war finished it seems nobody is quite how they were before; we're all just ghosts of ourselves really. Aren't we?'

* * * *

On the way out Posie swung by Inspector Oats' office. Normally she wouldn't mind rubbing him up the wrong way, but she genuinely felt sorry about having used and abused his time and efforts tonight; and worse, she was going to have to lie about it all too.

She put her head around his door. He was reading a fishing magazine in the light of the dim regulation police desk-lamp and looking pleased with himself.

'I'm off home now, Inspector,' Posie trilled cheerfully.

'Ah, talkative was she? Got the details you were looking for?'

'Well,' Posie said regretfully. 'Actually, no. No, I can't say it was that helpful. And I think you're going to have to rip up that charge-sheet and let her go, too.'

Posie tried not to look at the Inspector's thunderous face. She continued mildly:

'Turns out she's *not* claiming benefits falsely. In fact, the War Office have been informed about the current, accurate situation. And it turns out she's not a blackmailer, either. I don't think my clients will press charges on that score; they won't want the publicity. The evidence isn't really strong enough. I'm so sorry to have wasted your time.'

The Inspector's face was turning puce and he looked as if he wanted to get out of his chair and throttle Posie. She got in before he did:

'So it *was* a mare's nest, sir, after all. Sorry about that, and Merry Christmas to you and yours. Have a very pleasant evening.'

* * * *

Sixteen

The next day Posie sent a jolly little Christmas postcard featuring a nice fat robin red-breast to Mr Florizel at the Wickham Academy. The card was a bit odd as the bird was shown eating a worm, but it suited her purposes perfectly.

She sent it first-class by Saturday post, to arrive that evening. Valerie Florizel looked, just like Felicity Fyne, to be the possessive, jealous type and would no doubt have a problem with Dr Winter receiving the card no matter what, so Posie kept her message short and sweet.

It said, simply but cryptically:

Mr F,
  I caught the worm!
  All the best for the future,
  P.P

Posie sent Felicity a telegram too, telling her that she didn't have to worry about changing her window display of hats for Christmas Eve, that all was well. Posie also promised to come up to Hampstead in the afternoon.

Posie decided that she would go and walk up on

Hampstead Heath after she had visited Felicity's shop, to blow away the cobwebs and try and make this trip up to north London as nice as possible for herself.

Being the last day before Christmas when the shops were open, Hampstead Village High Street was busy, and its little boutiques were bustling with trade.

Posie found Felicity's shop easily. 'Very Fyne Hats' was a smart, glossily-painted affair sandwiched between a stylish dress shop and a gentleman's outfitters.

Rather than being the sterile place she had imagined, Posie was surprised to see it was painted a bright canary yellow inside, and it looked cheerful and fashionable. An old-fashioned curved bay window was carefully dressed with a few well-chosen cloche hats and small sprigs of silver-lacked holly and mistletoe were artfully displayed around the place. When she pushed open the door and the shop-bell rang out, Posie saw that custom was good, and perhaps five or six women were buying or ordering hats for the festive season. A wispy salesgirl with very short shingled hair and a dress in the current flapper style was modelling various styles of fancy hat for a couple of middle aged women with perhaps more money than dress sense.

Posie caught sight of Felicity at once, in her usual immaculate black, her hair looped up into a smart bun on top of her head. She was over near the back counter with a customer, wrapping something in bright yellow tissue paper. She saw Posie and nodded almost invisibly at her, indicating her to wait a few minutes.

On the tram ride up from the Kingsway Posie had thought a good deal about what to say to Felicity, how much of the truth to tell her. She remembered Dr Winter's words to her:

'Tell her some sort of version of the truth, if you must, Parker. But not where I am. Got it?'

She had decided on a version which was true enough, but which would hurt the least. But it had to be the truth.

When it came to playing with peoples' lives you couldn't afford to lie.

Posie stood to one side, trying on this hat and that. It was a shame she'd already bought her red hat for the winter; she couldn't really justify another one just yet. And anyhow, she still wasn't sure if she'd buy it from Felicity Fyne or not. It wasn't as if they had become pals over this strange case.

After ten minutes Felicity came over. The last customer had gone and the fashionable salesgirl had retreated to a back room somewhere. The shop was empty. Felicity quickly put the 'CLOSED' sign up on the door.

'Tell me…' she whispered, turning back into the shop, looking intently at Posie, her navy eyes wide with fear.

'Well, the good news is that I've caught the blackmailer, and they won't be contacting you again.'

'Ah, er, excellent. And my husband? What of him?'

Posie took a deep breath. She started with her 'some sort of version of the truth'.

'He *is* alive, Felicity. I can't lie to you. You didn't see a ghost. But he's not your Dr Winter anymore; he's someone else, someone you wouldn't recognise. I don't advise telling you any more of the details. But legitimately, in my view, you are entitled to keep receiving your pension; you don't need to inform anyone of anything. The man you were married to no longer exists. However, if you were to get married again, you would *legally* be committing bigamy, so I don't advise it.'

Felicity stared and stared.

'I told you, I'll never marry again. But I don't under-stand.'

I don't want you to understand, thought Posie ruefully to herself, willing Felicity not to ask her any more questions. She bit her lip and held Felicity's frightened gaze. If Felicity pressed her for more details, as was her right, Posie would have to be more forthcoming. As it was, she was walking a tightrope.

'Okay. I don't want all the details,' Felicity said at last. 'I can tell on your face that the news isn't good. I'm imagining he's lost his mind or sitting in an asylum and doesn't remember who I am or something. So it's better to think he died an honourable death. But tell me one thing,' Felicity breathed, 'is he married to someone else?'

Posie took a deep breath and then shook her head. 'Legally he's still married to you.' That much was true; the legal bit, anyhow.

Felicity laughed almost hysterically. 'I don't know what outcome I was expecting,' she said. 'This whole thing has been so odd that I would have believed almost anything. Thank you for your help. Send me your bill in the New Year please.'

Posie felt like she was being dismissed, like some sort of cheap tradesman or delivery boy. She smiled to herself, glad to leave for her breath of fresh air up on the Heath.

'Oh,' said Felicity, turning at the door. 'You never told me who the blackmailer was? Someone I knew in the war and annoyed somehow, I guess? Who was it?'

Posie grimaced. 'I'd rather not say. It's part of a deal I brokered. But, no. You'd never met them before.'

'So my husband knew them, then?'

'Very briefly. Another lifetime ago.'

Felicity turned the sign over in the door to reopen the shop and in the light of the bright day Posie's pink ring sparkled and caught the light of the window a few hundred times over.

'Oh, goodness me. Congratulations! An engagement!' trilled Felicity, holding the door back for Posie. But there was still that strange detachment, like she was not really meaning what she was saying.

'How things can change in a week!' blinked Felicity as the strong winter sunshine suddenly bathed her pale face in its unforgiving white light. 'Change is a good thing. For both of us. I do hope you'll be very happy.'

So do I, thought Posie.
So do I.

* * * *

NEW YEAR'S EVE 1922

Epilogue

Christmas came and went, and apart from one small Christmas caper involving a stuffed Polar Bear, their stay at Rebburn Abbey was just as delightful and cold and draughty as Posie had imagined it would be.

Alaric and Posie had announced their engagement to Rufus and Dolly first, who were thrilled at the news, and then in *The Times*, with a formal announcement.

'But it will just be a quiet wedding,' Posie told anyone who would listen. Dolly rolled her eyes and made faces behind Posie's back, already planning out what Posie should wear, and who should make her dress.

On their arrival back in London on Friday the 29th, Posie called in quickly at the Grape Street Bureau unannounced. Mainly this was to see her beloved Mr Minks, who had been cared for by the porter of her nearby block of flats in her absence. Posie was still wearing her thick travelling clothes, which was just as well as the office was freezing and Prudence, frugal as ever, hadn't bothered to light a fire just for herself.

Posie's office was full of flowers and congratulatory cards from well-wishers. She found Prudence already hard at work fending off phone calls from journalists: Alaric alone sold papers, but news of an engagement was top-drawer news. Prudence had started to keep a scrap-book full of press clippings about the happy couple.

'But when will the wedding be?' asked Prudence, beside herself with excitement.

'I have no idea. Honestly,' said Posie, almost bored of the fuss already, and stroking Mr Minks a few hundred times over. For once he seemed genuinely pleased to see her. 'There's a good deal to sort out.'

Posie waded through the piles of cards which had heaped up and had found one, in red handwriting, unobtrusively requesting Posie's presence at a New Year's Eve choral concert in Cambridge. She decided she would definitely attend.

'Oh, I almost forgot,' said Prudence, busily taking down Christmas cards and tinsel and throwing everything into a box, 'I took a call earlier from *Chief* Inspector Lovelace. He sends his congratulations to you, of course, but he wanted to thank you for the card and presents you sent to little Phyllis in the hospital. He was very touched. Wanted to tell you they've had a ropey old Christmas but she's turned a corner now and is definitely on the mend. She's back home again with them now, too.'

'What a relief. Poor little mite. Brrr. It's cold in here. Can't you light the bally fire? Hang the expense, for goodness' sake.'

The weather in London had turned bright and frightfully cold. It was frosty too but too cold for snow; proper Christmas weather, albeit late.

Just as Posie was getting ready to leave the office and bundling herself up in her many layers in the waiting room, there was a knock at the office door.

'Come in,' called out Prudence, without paying much attention. She was pinning bills together at her desk, a favourite activity.

Posie looked up to check her reflection in the big mirror which hung above the fireplace, and as she did so she looked backwards and caught sight of a woman entering the room through the glass door. She looked away again as she didn't recognise the woman and busied herself fixing her lipstick. *Honolulu Bay* today.

She almost dropped the golden lipstick cylinder when she heard the voice, which was familiar.

'I have something for Miss Parker. Can you see she gets it please?'

Posie swung around, lowering her big shawl and the thick tweed hat which had been obscuring her face.

'*Felicity?*'

Felicity Fyne looked over at Posie and smiled in a surprised fashion, a black and yellow hat-box raised mid-air. 'Oh, hullo Posie. I didn't see you there under all that… all that…all that…'

'Wool?'

'Quite. You look quite the hobo. Are you in hiding from the press?'

Felicity smiled archly.

'I've never been here before, you know. It took me a little while to find your office, up this dingy dark alley; I kept thinking I was in the wrong place. Anyway, I brought you something to say thank you for your help, and congratulations. I read about your engagement in the paper. You are a dark horse! Alaric Boynton-Dale, no less! This gift is a mere trifle. But perhaps it will suit you better than your, er, current *ensemble* does.'

Posie gulped, half-embarrassed, half-cross. But mainly she was shocked.

She was shocked at the woman herself.

The widow's weeds were gone. The rosary beads were absent. Felicity Fyne was wearing head-to-toe canary yellow, and her silver blonde hair had been shingled off into the very shortest of bobs. A slash of fuchsia lipstick completed the look. The overall effect was of some sort of tropical bird perched on a twig. Felicity Fyne had obviously decided to live again. Even if she wasn't looking for a marriage.

'Happy New Year Felicity,' Posie managed to say without looking like anything was amiss.

'I hope it will be a good one for you.'

* * * *

The concert in Cambridge was, as before, spectacular. It was New Year's Eve, a Sunday afternoon.

Dressed in her very best fur coat, and with a neat blue velvet hat perched on top of her head which almost exactly matched the colour of her eyes, courtesy of 'Very Fyne Hats', Posie felt she looked her very best for meeting her new nephew again.

And this time Posie managed to have a quick snatched tea with Harry, too, which was wonderful. Leaving him and Evangeline was hard; particularly as there was no way of knowing when they would be able to meet again.

After the tea and as the light was falling Posie walked down the road to Trinity College, where she had stayed so recently, but which felt like a lifetime ago.

She stood at the main gate and snatched a quick look at the beautiful old Great Court, rain-drenched and empty of students and visitors but now bathed in a beautiful orange evening light.

Who knew how long it would be before she came back here, or what would have happened by then? Perhaps she would meet Harry Eden Greenwood again, either here or in London, but nothing in life was certain, and it was too much for Evangeline to promise anything right now; she couldn't risk it, for Harold was suspicious of everything.

Posie understood, but it made her sad.

Suddenly she froze, all the hairs standing up on the back of her shingled neck:

'Nosy! Nosy Parker!'

She turned quickly. She thought she had heard someone call out that old, old nickname across the huge, echoing courtyard. Her brother's nickname for her. She caught sight of a figure standing by Richard's old stairway in the near distance, watching her, silhouetted against the setting orange sun.

Her heart lurched in her throat, for the man's silhouette was achingly familiar. Tall, but slightly stooped, as if to take up less room that he actually did, the man was wearing a scholar's gown and holding a wedge of untidy papers under his arm, and shielding his eyes with his right hand to get a better view of Posie, as if staring into a very bright light.

Richard.

It was Richard!

Posie was on the verge of shouting out her brother's name when she realised her mistake. Looking again she saw that there was no one there; just a mass of wet, shadowy, flame-coloured reflections against the stonework. It had just been a trick of the light. A hope.

A couple of newly-arrived students for the upcoming term were shouting at each other across the courtyard, their voices echoing strangely off the stones, and it had been their voices she had heard, warped and unclear.

Shaken more than she liked to admit, Posie picked up her bag and scurried along the glistening stone walkways in the shadows of the walls of the old quad, chastising herself for her momentary lapse of reason: there were no such thing as ghosts, and she had proved that firmly once and for all with this strange little case involving Dr Winter. If it had proved anything, the case had proved that a rational explanation lay behind almost everything.

Posie reached the Porter's Lodge and was about to pass through onto the street outside unobserved, quietly on her way back to catch the London train, when she remembered that she had received an important steer in the case from the friendly Porter, Simpkins. And he had led her to Harry, too, whether or not he had known the truth about Richard's son or not. She ought to thank him, and at the very least wish him a happy New Year.

Posie rapped on the glass divide in the Porter's Lodge, but she could see that the cosy little room inside was empty, and that people had been busy taking down the festive decorations, all of which had carefully been placed in an old tin box which was now sitting on the desk by the pigeonholes, ready to be stored away again for the next twelve months. When she looked again she saw a familiar-looking box of chocolates from All Saints Passage sitting on the desk, too.

Posie tapped again, harder this time, and at last an elderly-looking Porter came out from the back room with a cup of tea in his hands, apologising profusely.

'Absolutely no problem.' Posie smiled. 'I'm after Simpkins, actually. I wanted to express my thanks to him. He helped me with something rather difficult, actually. I wouldn't have got far without him. But he's not on duty today?'

The Porter was looking at Posie strangely. As if she might not be quite right in the head.

'Knew him, did you, Miss?'

'No. I just said: he helped me out with a problem I had. That's all…'

'Was this recently, Miss?'

'Oh yes. Just before Christmas. Not two weeks ago. Can you pass on a message, then?'

The Porter shook his head slowly, guardedly. 'No, that I can't do, Miss. I'm very sorry to have to tell you that the Porter you are referring to, Stan Simpkins, has died.'

Posie was stunned. 'Oh! I'm so very sorry. Was it very sudden? How terrible. And he was no age at all! Thirty! If a day! What a shock for his family!'

She picked her bag up, genuinely sad, and turned to go, but the elderly Porter had come through the small doorway and was standing by Posie's side, as if trying to make up his mind about something. He pointed quickly, as if embarrassed, to a small wooden plaque set carefully and unobtrusively into the wooden panels of the surrounds. Surprised, Posie scanned the short list of five gold-stencilled names in the wood and she gasped aloud.

The plaque was a small memorial to the Porters of Trinity College Cambridge who had died in the First World War, and the first two names were those of Stan Simpkins and Frank Bevans, who had both died on the same day, in 1916.

Posie stared uncomprehendingly, her heart ricocheting in her chest, and then she looked at the elderly Porter, as if for an explanation. Again, she had the unpleasant feeling of hairs standing up on her neck. The Porter shrugged and took a sip of his tea, as if for reassurance.

'It's happened before,' he said in a slightly puzzled tone. 'But we just thought the person reporting meeting Stan was a bit barmy.'

Posie swallowed hard. 'What was he like, Stan Simpkins?'

'To look at? Nothing special, poor lad. Dark. Big ears. I've a photograph here…'

The Porter passed a photo through the divide to Posie and she shivered as she realised she had seen it before. It was the cricket photo from 1913, featuring her brother Richard, and now that she looked hard, she recognised Stan Simpkins too, sitting happily on the bottom row. He had been grinning from ear to ear and was wearing a hand-knitted white tank-top which looked way too large for him.

'He loved his job, Stan did,' the Porter continued. 'Lived for it! He loved helping out. He liked getting to the bottom of problems. Couldn't do enough for people. He got on with everyone: visitors, students, the academic staff. We were all gutted when we heard about his death. Some who work here think Stan's still here, haunting the place; almost as if he still wants to carry on like he did before. Some think his pal, Frank Bevans, haunts the place too. But that's less likely. They never found his body, I'm told: so how could he appear as a ghost? But I don't believe in ghosts anyway. Load of nonsense. Stuff and nonsense.'

Posie stared at the man, utterly speechless, knowing she should be horrified and scared stiff but all she felt was a strange sort of calm, an inevitability. When she spoke, the words which came were almost unbelievably trivial:

'Just a minor point, but the open box of chocolates on the desk there…who do they belong to?'

The Porter flushed a dark red. 'Not yours, were they, Miss? Sorry if that's the case… But we found them, our team, the week before Christmas. No note or explanation was with them, they were just sitting on our desk. We assumed they were a Christmas present from a grateful Professor or someone who didn't want to draw attention to themselves. And such a large box, too. They must have cost the earth…we've still got a couple left over. Want one, do you?'

Posie shook her head and as she came out onto Trinity Street, she exhaled deeply. She tried to shake off the shivery cold feeling her last encounter had left her with, but she didn't succeed. Instead she shrugged her chin down further into her fur coat and took a brisk step out into the darkness in the direction of the train station and London.

Posie hurried along, desperate to leave. She gave herself a tough talking-to. She didn't believe in ghosts. Couldn't. She didn't have the time or energy or inclination for them. Besides, tomorrow was 1923, and all the rough edges left by the war would have no place there. They would have to stay firmly in the past.

Also, on a more cheerful note, Alaric would be waiting

in London at the Criterion for her, and she would banish thoughts of this strange afternoon by dancing to a new kind of music she had heard would be on the programme; something incomprehensible but exciting called jazz.

But she needed to eat something first.

She remembered the chocolate shop in All Saints Passage and decided to take a quick detour past it. Hopefully she'd find it open, catering for the tourist trade. A large box of chocolates would be perfect for the train-ride home; a veritable supper in fact.

And this time, sure as bread was bread, she wouldn't be giving them away. Not to anyone.

Alive or dead.

* * * *

Thanks for joining Posie Parker.

Enjoyed *The Vanishing of Dr Winter* (A Posie Parker Mystery #4)? Here's what you can do next.

If you loved this book and have a tiny moment to spare I would really appreciate a short review on the page where you bought the book. Your help in spreading the word about the series is invaluable and really appreciated, and reviews make a big difference to helping new readers find the series.

Posie's previous cases are all available in e-book and paperback formats from Amazon, as well as in selected bookstores.

You can find all of the previous books, available for purchase, listed here in chronological order:

www.amazon.com/L.B.-Hathaway/e/
B00LDXGKE8 and

www.amazon.co.uk/L.B.-Hathaway/e/B00LDXGKE8

More Posie Parker books will be released in late 2016.

You can sign up to be notified of new releases, pre-release specials, free short stories and the chance to win Amazon gift-vouchers here:

www.lbhathaway.com/contact/newsletter/

Historical Note

The characters in this novel are all fictional. However, the historical timings, weather, dates, general background and detail described are accurate to the best of my knowledge, save for the following exceptions:

1. The chocolate shop in All Saints Passage, Cambridge, is fictional. There was no chocolate shop there (to the best of my knowledge) in 1922. However, it *is* based on a wonderful and unique chocolate shop, Bellina, which was located in All Saints Passage for many years, until its relocation in 2007 to another nearby street. See: http://www.chocolatehouse.co.uk

2. Fitzbillies on Trumpington Street, Cambridge, did open in 1922, but closed in 2014. It was famous for its Chelsea buns. I have made it into a tea room in this story, whereas in real life it was rather a shop which sold cakes over the counter.

3. I have played with dates with regard to Merlin, Benny's police dog in the ambulance unit: although German Shepherd dogs were introduced in England at the end of the nineteenth century, they were used in the *Second* World War on the front line of battle, rather than in the First (or Great) War.

4. The Casualty Clearing Station (CCS) I describe is entirely fictional. However, CCS Number 8 *was* active in real life between 5 March 1917 and 15 April 1918. Rather than being located exactly at Arras itself (as in this story) it was at Agnez-les-Duisans, *near* Arras. CCS Number 8 was unusual in existing where it did for a relatively long time (see the short note below) making it a semi-permanent medical outpost. Please note that the characters working at this CCS as described in this story are entirely fictional, as is the bombing of the place.

A Short Note on Casualty Clearing Stations (CCSs)

These were always near the front line in the Great War of 1914–18. A CCS was not a 'real' hospital, but represented a stopping-off-point between the actual warzone and a fully-equipped field hospital. Stacks of men were brought through a CCS to be patched up, operated on, or simply to be given the all-clear. Sometimes men died there in vast numbers.

CCSs were normally made up of canvas tents and a few huts, but were sometimes located in more permanent buildings. Each CCS had a medical team or unit of doctors, surgeons, nurses, orderlies and Red Cross volunteers.

CCSs often moved according to where the fighting was, and were therefore temporary by nature. They were also very susceptible to dangerous attacks by shelling, gunfire and gas and had to be able to move at a moment's notice.

Today the position of many CCSs can be located in France and Belgium on the former front lines of battle due to the cemeteries which inevitably grew up there. A useful list of the CCSs can be found here: http://www.vlib.us/medical/CCS/ccs.htm#Top

5. The Lion d'Or in Arras is fictional.

6. The *SS Victoria* and its sinking by a U-boat in the English Channel on Christmas Eve 1917 is fictional.

7. The famous and chilling murder case (involving Edith Thompson and Freddie Bywaters) which gripped the nation in 1922 and which the Porter is reading about at Trinity College was indeed real, but the suspects had already been found guilty by 18th December 1922 (the verdict was given on the 11th December).

8. Eaden Lilley's and Robert Sayle's (where Posie buys Christmas presents) were two established Department Stores in Cambridge in 1922. Both have now gone.

9. The Department of Botany at the University of Cambridge is now the Department of Plant Sciences, but geographically it remains in the same place as its 1920s incarnation.

10. The Imperial War Graves Commission as mentioned is now the Commonwealth War Graves Commission.

11. Geographically, I have played with the location of the Zeppelin raid in Soho. There was never a Zeppelin raid on Rupert Street, but there was one on nearby Piccadilly Circus at the same time as detailed in the story (19th October 1917) with a loss of seven lives and huge destruction to the area. There were several Zeppelin raids in central London (including in Soho) during the Great War. The damage left by them was indeed visible for years afterwards in the London landscape, with bomb craters and hoardings covering the bomb-sites remaining visible throughout the 1920s.

12. 'The Florence' Restaurant on Rupert Street was a fashionable and popular restaurant set up during the Victorian era, running on through the Great War into the 1920s and 1930s. Run by Luigi Azario, it was something of a celebrity hotspot and Oscar Wilde was one of its famous early patrons. It no longer exists and its premises now belong to a mobile phone shop.

13. The nurses' hostel as detailed in this story (on Rupert Street) is fictional, although women's hostels were abundant all over London at this time, especially in Soho and the area around the Tottenham Court Road.

14. The Wickham Academy for Boys at Bishop's Stortford is fictional, as is the River Wick.

15. Posie's black Brigg umbrella is from Swaine Adeney Brigg. See: http://www.swaineadeneybrigg.com/

16. The Geddes Axe, or Geddes Act which Mr Florizel refers to in Chapter Eleven (and is mentioned too by Chief Inspector Lovelace in Chapter Seven) was a programme of major cuts in public spending implemented by David Lloyd George's government during the course of 1921-1922. Britain was crippled by huge debts following the Great War (national debt was £7.8 billion by 1920, which was larger than the country's GDP) but the spending cuts which were instigated hit people very hard and contributed to Britain's downturn in the next decade. One of the major areas to be affected by the Geddes Axe was education, with teachers' salaries being slashed by 8 shillings per week (£58 in todays' money) in 1922.

17. The Triumph Motorbike as ridden by Alaric Boynton-Dale in Chapter Thirteen would have been made

by Triumph Engineering in 1922, rather than the current manufacturer of the bikes, Triumph Motorcycles Ltd, which is a separate company.

18. The terms 'blackmail' and 'blackmailer' were in colloquial use in England in 1922, but in legal terms it had no standing until the 1960's. Instead, a blackmailer in the 1920's would have been tried for crimes of extortion or 'menaces' under the *Larceny Act* of 1916, as Inspector Oats refers to in Chapter Fourteen, and which I've glossed over in Chapter Fifteen to keep things easier for the modern reader.

EPILOGUE

19. There is no such plaque in the current Porter's Lodge.

* * * *

Recipe for World War One Ginger Cake*

*This is a 1916 Scottish recipe for Ginger Sponge Cake as originally featured in *The Falkirk Herald*.

The slightly modern adjustments are courtesy of Laura Macdonald, who rediscovered the recipe. She writes a cookery blog at www.yellowbrolly.co.uk. Laura can also be found on twitter @TheYellowBrolly.

In addition, she made a wonderful film (see link below) all about baking this very cake, and it features some interesting background about rationing of food in World War One Britain, too. Definitely worth a peep. www.scottisharchives.org.uk/ediblearchive/ww1

RECIPE

1. Take a half pound of golden syrup, two ounces of butter, one egg, half an ounce of ground ginger, ten ounces of flour, two ounces of sugar, about two tablespoons of milk and half a teaspoon of soda.

2. Put the flour, ginger and sugar into a bowl.

3. In a saucepan, stir the milk, butter and syrup until dissolved, then stir in the dry ingredients.

4. Dissolve the soda in a little milk, add this and the well-beaten egg to the mixture, pour into a shallow tin lined with greased paper and bake for thirty or forty minutes in a slow oven.

5. Cut into fingers when cold.

6. Laura recommends using finely grated fresh ginger rather than ground, and substituting self-raising flour for plain and bicarbonate soda. She suggests the cake should be baked at 180 degrees for 30 minutes.

Acknowledgements
and Author Note

1. Thank you to the Master and Fellows of Trinity College, Cambridge, for allowing me to use Trinity College as a location in this story.

2. Thank you to *The Falkirk Herald* for allowing me to use its original 1916 recipe for Ginger Sponge Cake and thanks too to Laura Macdonald (www.yellowbrolly.co.uk) for rediscovering the 1916 Ginger Sponge Cake recipe in the first place and for helping with the slight adjustments in the recipe.

3. Thank you to the author Nathan Dylan Goodwin, whose brain I have picked on occasion regarding this book and whose bestselling book, *The Orange Lilies*, inspired me to revisit Posie Parker's own World War One experience in the first place. I also owe him the reference to the Christmas goodie tins sent out from the Royal family to the troops on the front line.

http://www.amazon.com/The-Orange-Lilies-Forensic-Genealogist-ebook/dp/B00QF7HXAW

4.   I personally dislike heavy quotations at the start of books, and I don't think they would be quite right in the Posie Parker Mystery series. However, Shakespeare's *The Winter's Tale* features quite often in this story. If I were to quote something from it, it would be this:

"What's gone and what's past help should be past grief." (*The Winter's Tale*, Act 3.2).

My supremely unworthy translation of this is: "No point crying over spilt milk. Move on."

And I think that's just what Posie Parker would have said about her experiences in the Great War, however awful.

Further Reading

1. The classic reading for the experience of a young female volunteer nurse on the front line in the Great War of 1914–18 (and all the tragedy it entailed) is of course Vera Brittain's wonderful, harrowing autobiography, *Testament of Youth*.

    See: http://www.amazon.com/Testament-Youth-Autobiographical-Study-1900-1925-ebook/dp/B002U3CCH4/ref=asap_bc?ie=UTF8

2. Other interesting books I found useful in the research for this novel were:

    a. *War Girls: The First Aid Nursing Yeomanry in the First World War,* by Janet Lee (Manchester University Press, 2012 Reprint). See:

        http://www.amazon.com/War-Girls-First-Nursing-Yeomanry/dp/0719067138/edwardiannovelist-20

    b. *Elsie and Mairi Go to War: Two Extraordinary Women on the Western Front*, by Diane Atkinson (Preface Publishing, 2010 edition). See:

http://www.amazon.com/Elsie-Mairi-Go-War-Extraordinary/dp/1848091354/ref=pd_sim_sbs_14_2?ie=UTF8&refRID=0VREZXE0H8BCNN3B6E77

c. *Women in the War Zone: Hospital Service in the First World War*, by Anne Powel (The History Press, 2013). See:

http://www.amazon.com/Women-War-Zone-Hospital-Service/dp/0752493604/ref=pd_sim_14_2?ie=UTF8&refRID=1VS970AT7Y0XDSBF67N2

About the Author

Cambridge-educated, British-born L.B. Hathaway writes historical fiction and contributes to a number of popular history magazines and websites. She worked as a lawyer at Lincoln's Inn in London for almost a decade before becoming a full-time writer. She is a lifelong fan of detective novels set in the Golden Age of Crime, and is an ardent Agatha Christie devotee.

Her other interests, in no particular order, are: very fast downhill skiing, theatre-going, drinking strong tea, Tudor history, exploring castles and generally trying to cram as much into life as possible. She lives in London and Switzerland with her husband and young family.

The Posie Parker series of cosy crime novels and novellas span the 1920s. They each combine a core central mystery, an exploration of the reckless glamour of the age and a feisty protagonist who you would love to have as your best friend.

To find out more and for news of new releases and giveaways, go to:

http://www.lbhathaway.com

Connect with L.B. Hathaway online:

(e) author@lbhathaway.com

(t) @LbHathaway

(f) https://www.facebook.com/pages/L-B-Hathaway-books/1423516601228019

(Goodreads)   http://www.goodreads.com/author/show/8339051.L_B_Hathaway

34422723R00134

Printed in Great Britain
by Amazon